THE GHOST OF WITCH'S POINT

THE GHOST OF WITCH'S POINT

R.W. HARRISON

Excerpt from *The Search for Bridey Murphy* used by permission. *The Search for Bridey Murphy*, Morey Bernstein, Penguin Random House, 2002 (orig. 1956).

ISBN: 9798358820456

CHAPTER ONE

Wilbur stood at the base of the lighthouse, beaming at the small family of tourists in front of him. "Witch's Point Lighthouse was built in 1881 and stands just under one hundred feet tall. It marks the entrance to the harbor and warns ships that there are rocky shoals just offshore. It's tricky to navigate, especially for ships coming from the south, and before she was built, there were more than three dozen wrecks here—that we know about. There were probably a lot more that were never reported. And here we are in 1960, seventy-nine years later, and she's still protecting the harbor faithfully. "

He leaned down and picked up a brick from the ground. "Over seventeen thousand of these were used in the lighthouse's construction, and it took almost two years to complete." As he continued with the history, he noticed the father stifle a yawn and glance at his watch. He skipped the part about how President

James Garfield was to dedicate the lighthouse on the Fourth of July, but had been shot by an assassin just two days earlier. Instead, the lieutenant governor of the state came, but the assembled crowd was much smaller than originally anticipated.

"Now, before we go in, a word of caution. The stairs are steep, so please be careful, and use the handrail at all times."

"Can you see through the stairs, Mister…?" the wife asked, her face twisted into a frightened grimace.

"Philpott. Wilbur Philpott."

"I have a problem with stairs where I can see through the gaps," she continued. She turned to her husband before Wilbur could answer. "Ed, what are those things called?" she asked, turning her hand sideways and moving it up and down.

"Risers, Eleanor. Risers."

"Oh yes, those things. If I can see through the risers, I don't think I can go up. I hope they're not rickety either. Because if—"

Wilbur held up his hand. "They're not made of wood, ma'am. The steps are made of solid stone. Granite all the way up."

"Oh, that makes me feel better. Thank you."

"One other thing. There are two landings on the way to the top. Both are stone platforms that lead out to open windows. So, please, no crawling on the landings toward those windows. Wouldn't want my littlest guest to fall out, right?" he said, winking at the boy, who looked to be around ten.

Wilbur sighed inwardly when he saw Ed roll his

eyes, but he opened the metal door with a flourish, ushering the group inside. The air was cool and dank and he noticed the wife crinkle her nose at the musty smell.

"You're now standing at the bottom of the tallest lighthouse in the state, ninety-nine feet from here to the very top. Anyone care to guess how many steps?"

"Ten thousand?" the boy offered with a smirk.

"Simon, be nice," his mother admonished.

Wilbur laughed. "It may seem like that, especially if you've climbed them as many times as I have, but no, not quite that many. Anyone else?"

"Two hundred?" the wife suggested.

"Very close. It's actually—"

"One hundred and thirty-nine," Ed said.

"Precisely. That was a very good guess," Wilbur said with a smile.

"It was on the brochure in our hotel lobby."

"Oh, yes, of course." He turned to the first of the hundred and thirty-nine steps and pointed out the steep climb to the first one. "Here we go. Watch that first step and remember to hold on to the railing."

Wilbur led the family up the steps, reciting some more of the history of the lighthouse. He hoped he could interest Ed, but he seemed more like a fellow who wanted to make good time on the interstate and not be bothered with smaller tourist attractions like this. Stopping halfway to the first landing, he turned around to check on the group.

"Everybody doing okay? It's easy at first, but if you're not used to the climb, it'll be tough at the top."

"We're fine," Ed said, the impatience tight in his voice.

Wilbur stopped again at the first landing and pointed out the window. "We're only about thirty feet up, but you get a delightful view of the water from here. And on a breezy day like this, you can lick your lips and taste the salt." He watched with delight as the boy and Ed's wife did just that. He opened his eyes a bit in surprise when Ed darted his tongue out and over his lips.

"If you'd like to sit on the landing, go ahead, just stay close." Now was the time to entice Simon. "Let me share with you something that isn't in the brochure." He leaned down and in a voice just above a whisper, he said, "The lighthouse is haunted."

"Whoa!" the boy said. "Really?"

"Oh, yes."

"Dad, did you hear that? It's haunted!"

"Uh huh," Ed replied, the boredom in his voice now quite apparent.

"Really, Mister Philpott?" Eleanor asked, clearly not sure if this was something to be believed or not.

He nodded gravely. "The story goes that the original lighthouse keeper, a gentleman by the name of Bartholomew Stern, failed to light the lamp one night back in 1898. He had been known to imbibe a little too much, and it was here, at this spot, that he passed out. He never made it to the top of the light."

All three of the visitors looked around at the landing, and Wilbur could tell he was winning over at least the boy and his mother, if not the father.

"A terrible storm whipped up later that night," he continued. "It was a nor'easter like there ever was one. Waves were estimated at forty feet and the winds howled down the coastline at seventy miles an hour. The tips of the waves were frothy with spray and the water churned and heaved like an enormous, angry teapot."

Even Ed, the father, seemed rapt by his tale, fascinated by every word.

"A mile out to sea, the *Yarmouth*, a schooner from Halifax, saw the faint lights of the town you drove through to get here and made for land. The captain was a tough-as-nails seaman from Salem named Merritt Holland who had sailed around Cape Horn eleven times. And he had no idea they were headed directly toward the rocks."

Wilbur pointed out the narrow window to the ocean. "He started his turn to land just out there, and you can see the rocks from here. But, of course, it was dark and there was no light. The *Yarmouth* sailed through the inky black water toward their destruction. Neither the captain, nor his crew of eight, knew what was coming."

He paused to build the suspense. "The boat hit the rocks with a terrific crash," he said, smacking his hands together. "The bow ripped open and water gushed inside. With the wind still blowing against the sails, the masts snapped. There was no saving her and the captain called for his men to abandon ship. The screams of the men surrounded him in the darkness, some from on deck from those who hadn't been thrown overboard, and others were from below, trapped and drowning."

"How terrible," the mother said, peering out the window at the tumble of boulders just half a mile from shore.

Wilbur continued, confident that even Ed was fully engaged in the story. "As much as the captain was heartbroken by the screams from below, it was the cries of his wife that affected him the most. There were reports she was from Salem also and had been driven out of town for the hex she placed on her first husband. He ran to her in their cabin, but an enormous wave heaved the ship over—and through—the rocks toward the small beach there. There was chaos everywhere as more men were flung overboard. What he didn't hear anymore were the men below. They had perished. He shouted to two men he could see in the water, urging them on to the shore as they clung onto pieces of the planking."

He paused again, making sure his small audience was paying attention. If he told the story like he always did, with just the right emphasis and cadence, he could usually hook everyone. Even someone like Ed.

"The cabin door was jammed shut, the ship almost on its side, and Captain Holland's wife was screaming as water rushed in. He threw his weight into it once, twice, three times, and finally it burst open. He dashed inside, scooped up his wife, and ran as best he could across the listing deck. The ship was disintegrating around him with each crashing wave, and he had no choice but to leap off the side with her. Barely keeping his head above the pounding surf, he swam mightily toward the shore, pulling his beloved behind him through the water. After a heroic effort, he finally dragged himself and his wife to the sand. She was breathing, but barely."

He stopped and pointed up the steps. "Let's get up to the next landing and I'll finish the story."

Wilbur's timing was perfect as all three of his visitors protested with groans. They wanted to hear the rest now, but he knew how to give them their money's worth. When they reached the next window, he pointed out through it to the small spit of sand below.

"That's where the captain came ashore. He could see the silhouette of the lighthouse towering above him and, exhausted, he dragged his wife to the base. Once inside and out of the wind and rain, he collapsed on the floor, right where you came in. He heard stirring up the stairs, right about where we're standing. 'Help me,' he called. Mr. Stern, the lightkeeper, was unsteady on his feet from drink and couldn't come down the stairs quickly enough, plus he was in no condition to render aid. The captain's wife died in his arms.

"Enraged and heartbroken, the captain charged up the steps until he met Mr. Stern at this very spot. He accused the keeper of murder, not only of his beloved wife, but of his crew—none of whom were ever found —because he failed to light the lamp. The empty bottle of whisky chose that moment to fall out of Mr. Stern's pocket. Seeing that, the captain grabbed him by his collar and, after a brief struggle, threw the man out this very window to his death. Now, it was known that

Mr. Stern liked his food as much as his drink, and was quite heavy, so it's a mystery how he managed it."

Both Ed and Eleanor gasped at the climax of the story and the boy's eyes were wide and his mouth hung open.

"The captain's wife has been trapped here ever since. That's why it's called Witch's Point Lighthouse and how it came to be haunted." Another pause. "And if you're really quiet, you might hear the voice of the lighthouse. Her voice. This is the perfect place to hear it."

CHAPTER TWO

The tourists stood still, looking around the interior, peering up and down the spiral staircase. There was no sound except the crashing of the waves against the rocks below. They remained silent for a full minute until the boy spoke up.

"I don't hear anything."

They were standing on the stone steps with Wilbur at the top, just past the landing. Next was Ed at the landing, then his son, and then Eleanor, who stood one step below. Wilbur put his finger to his mouth to urge them to be quiet so they could hear it. He cocked his head at the murmur and looked at the group with a quick nod of his head.

It was an indistinct sound, a hum almost, different from the wind and the waves. Wilbur nodded more vigorously, sure that the lighthouse wouldn't disappoint. He looked at his visitors, but none of them seemed to hear anything unusual.

Ed sighed heavily, the spell of the story apparently broken. "Okay, Mr. Philpott. Your little spook show is over. There's no ghost or witch here. Let's just finish up—"

"Dad, I heard—"

Before his son could finish his sentence, Ed fell backwards onto the narrow landing. He slid toward the open window, scrambling to find purchase against the smooth stone. "Hey! What the hell!"

An unseen force pulled—or pushed—him backwards, slowly, inexorably.

"Ed!" his wife shouted, reaching for him.

"Dad!"

Wilbur cleared his throat and grabbed the man's shoe, arresting his slide inches from the opening.

The man scrunched forward on the seat of his pants until he reached the steps. "Okay, what the fu— what was that?" he demanded, glaring at Wilbur.

"Sometimes the wind can catch you off balance, the way it whips through here. I've ended up right where you were on more than occasion."

"Wind, my ass, old man."

"Ed, stop that. He didn't do anything," Eleanor said, mouthing an apology to Wilbur.

"I don't know what kind of racket you've got here, but we're leaving," Ed said to him.

"Dad, I want to go to the top." The boy looked at Wilbur. "You said we could go all the way up, right?"

"That's right, son. That's what you paid for." Wilbur hoped to appeal to Ed's sense of frugality to continue the tour.

Ed looked trapped. He sighed and smoothed his shirt, glancing between his wife and the boy. He sighed again and shook his head. "Fine. Let's get this over with."

"Right this way," Wilbur said, leading them up the rest of the way to the metal hatch. Pushing hard against its rusty hinges, he flipped it back and stepped out onto the platform. "It's very windy up here, so please be careful," he called down. Reaching down, he took the hand of each of them, helping them onto the round balcony.

The wind coming off the ocean clawed at them and Wilbur gestured to the inner and outer railings. "Hold on to one of these, especially on the windward side. We'll take a slow walk all the way around so you can see the full three-sixty view, then we'll turn on the lamp."

From almost a hundred feet up, the view of the water and the shoreline was expansive. Wilbur watched and saw that Ed was back to enjoying himself as he pointed things out to his son. Eleanor didn't venture toward the outer railing, preferring to stay close to the inner stone column. Probably not too fond of heights, Wilbur guessed.

Simon pointed excitedly to a sailboat far out to sea, its white sail taut against the wind. Wilbur couldn't hear what he was saying, but he smiled at the joy the lighthouse was bringing at least one member of the family.

When they reached the leeward side of the platform, it was easier to hear one another and Wilbur didn't have to raise his voice as much. He held up a large key ring, clutching a large, old-fashioned key between his finger and thumb. "Here's where we go inside the lantern, folks." He inserted the key and twisted it, hearing the satisfying lock mechanism open, and pulled on the door.

"Every day, I clean the outside of the glass and give the Fresnel a once-over. That's the giant lens you see here. It's named after Augustin Jean Fresnel, who invented this beehive-looking glass that magnifies and reflects the light, making it brighter and more focused. It can be seen almost to the horizon. He never claimed a patent on his invention, giving this life-saving device freely to the world." He let the family walk around the lens, watching them take pictures and inspecting everything.

"You wash it every day?" Simon asked, his eyes wide.

Nodding, Wilbur led them back out the door, patting the lens affectionately. "She's been a faithful lighthouse for almost eighty years, and she deserves to be well taken care of."

A few steps back down into the lighthouse, he stopped at a door. "This is the motor room, which also houses the master switch. Who wants to turn on the light?"

"Can I do it? Dad, can I?"

Ed nodded with a small smile. "Sure. If it's okay with Mr. Philpott."

"Of course it is. Come on in. Only room for the two

of us, I'm afraid," he said, glancing at the boy's mother and father. "Won't take but a minute."

Ed nodded again, waving his son toward the open door.

Wilbur flipped on the light switch, illuminating the room, and motioned to the boy. "See that big switch on the wall? That's what you'll be flipping. It'll take two hands and you'll want to push it all the way until it clicks into place. There will be a loud noise when you do, but that's just the contacts in the motor. Push the switch all the way home and then do the same with this smaller switch. That's the light itself."

"Okay, I got it," the boy said, a grin spread wide across his face.

"Ready?"

"Yes, sir!" the boy exclaimed with a vigorous nod.

"One, two, three...now!" Wilbur said.

The boy thrust the switch upward, and the motor came to life with a bang, slowly rotating the heavy metal shaft. Then he switched on the light with equal enthusiasm.

"Well done, son. Let's go look, shall we?" Wilbur said.

They headed out of the motor room and back up through the hatch. Although it was still daylight, the powerful rotating light was unmistakable, cutting through the slight mist that reached to the top of the tower.

The boy shouted down to his parents. "Mom, Dad! Look, I did it!"

Ed and his wife stuck their heads through the hatch. "Nice job, Simon," Ed said.

Wilbur smiled at their excitement and guided them all back down. "Where are you folks headed after this?"

"Down the coast to New York City. Just thought we'd take a little detour before we got on the interstate."

"Well, I'll keep the light going for you." He looked at the boy. "Simon, you can look back and see it until it's out of sight and you'll know you're keeping ships at sea safe."

Simon's eyes grew wide again and he smiled at Wilbur and his dad.

Wilbur led the way down the stone steps, cautioning them again to hold on to the railing.

The boy stopped at the first landing and pointed to the interior of the tower, to the two metal crossbeams stretching from wall to wall. "What's that rope hanging there for?"

Wilbur rubbed his grizzled white beard and spoke in a somber voice. "You know, I don't quite know. It's been there a long time, that's for sure."

When they reached the bottom, Ed pulled Wilbur aside after his wife and son were out the door. "Listen, Mister Philpott, I'm sorry for blowing up at you earlier." He flipped his car keys around his finger, making a slight jingling sound.

"Don't worry a thing about it, sir," he replied. "It's forgotten."

The man glanced up at the short length of rope. "I have a feeling you know what that rope is, don't you?"

Wilbur nodded. "The captain was so despondent over the loss of his beloved wife that he hanged himself. He inched across the iron bars, tied a rope around the center, and slid off, directly over her dead body. That's where they cut him down. The piece of rope is what was left of the noose."

Ed leaned against the wall and rubbed the back of his neck. "So this whole story is true, not just something made up for the tourists? I mean, the place really is haunted?"

Wilbur pursed his lips and eyed him. He pointed to Ed's hand. "Did you feel any tingling when you held onto the railing on your way down?"

The man took a step forward, away from the wall, and turned toward the railing, placing his palm on the wrought iron. He shot his hand back and rubbed it against his pants, dropped his keys from his other hand, and stared at Wilbur.

"What the—" Ed stopped rubbing his palm and looked at his hand, shaking his head. "Wait a minute," he said. "If the lighthouse keeper was tossed to his death, and the wife died, and the captain hanged himself, how do you know all this?"

Before Wilbur could answer, Ed knelt down slowly to pick up his keys, his gaze still fixed on Wilbur. He glanced away to grab them and paused, tilting his head. "What's that?" he asked, pointing to something shiny in a crack in the mortar.

Wilbur leaned down and spotted something glinting in the light. "Hmm. I don't know." He lowered himself to the floor of the lighthouse and peered closer.

"It appears to be a piece of glass," he said. He grasped the edge and pulled it out. The moment he touched it, a long, low groan echoed through the lighthouse. The moan started from the top and wound its way down the steps, past the two men, and out the door.

Ed wasted no time in retrieving his keys and darted out the door. By the time Wilbur stepped outside, the family was halfway to their car.

CHAPTER THREE

Wilbur waved to the family as they drove out the gravel driveway to the road. A moment later, they had pulled onto the road and the sight of Simon waving to him warmed his heart.

He turned back to the lighthouse and ran a weathered hand through his gray hair. Gazing to the top and the slowly rotating beam, he chuckled. "You put on a good show today, old girl," he said. Spray from a wave crashing against a nearby rock reached him and he instinctively licked his lips.

He turned his attention to the half-inch long chip of glass in his palm. One edge was jagged, like it had been broken, but the other edge was curved and finished with what appeared to be a bead of tarnished silver. "Very curious," he said out loud. Turning back to the lighthouse, he said, "You never fail to surprise me."

Standing here in the shadow of the light, hearing the pounding surf and tasting the salt in the air, is what Wilbur lived for. Taking care of the old tower, and entertaining the occasional tourist, was exactly what he wanted in his retirement.

The sound of an approaching vehicle on the stones snapped him out of his reverie, and his shoulders sagged. He recognized the noise of his own truck approaching, his wife of thirty years at the wheel. Her trips into town had become more frequent and lasted longer over the last year or so. Their arguments came more often as well.

When she parked the truck, he ambled over to her to help with the groceries, but didn't see any, and she only exited with her purse.

"Hey, June Bug. Thought you were going to the supermarket," he said, trying to be upbeat.

"How many times have I told you it's just June? Not June Bug," she said, shaking her head. "You've got me hating my own name because all I hear is June Bug."

"I'm sorry, dear. You used to love it when we were dating." His tone was low and mournful. He so disliked when they quarreled. Why couldn't it be like when they were first married? he thought. Sure, he was older than her by twelve years, but back then she looked up to him, practically worshipped him for his wisdom and experience. He looked at his boots and his eyes glazed over as he recalled their wedding night when he carried her over the threshold to their room in Niagara Falls. They had giggled and talked and laughed together that whole week. Maybe a trip to the Falls would do them good. Rekindle what had been lost. It had been, what, almost thirty years since that magical week.

"June, what would you think about driving to—" He looked up but she had already gone inside. He sighed and trudged toward the house. Passing by the truck, he glanced inside and spotted a blue ball cap sitting on the floor of the passenger side. It had "Benson's Tires" embroidered on the front with greasy smudges on the bill.

He pulled open the screen door and entered the kitchen of the old house, his feet creaking along the worn wood floor. The bottom floor appeared to be empty, so she must be upstairs. "June B—" he called from the base of the stairs, catching himself. "June? Are you up there?"

He was met with silence, so he started up the steps. The carpet that ran up the middle of the stairs was threadbare in places and he knew that was another bone of contention with his wife. She wanted new carpet throughout the house, including the stairs, but he couldn't bear to cover up the hardwood.

Reaching the landing, Wilbur paused, still not hearing anything. Where could she have gone, he wondered. "June," he called again, starting toward their bedroom. When he reached the doorway, he saw her on the edge of the bed with the bedside phone to her ear. She was giggling quietly with a lilt in her voice that he hadn't heard in years.

He took a step into the room, and she turned to glare at him. "What do you want?" she barked. She turned back to the phone. "No, not you. I'm sorry. It was just Wilbur." There was a pause and she laughed. "I know. I'll talk to you later. Bye." She turned back to him. "Why are you always creeping around? Jesus!"

"I wasn't, dear. I came to find out if there was something wrong with the truck."

"Something wrong? No, why?"

"I saw a hat from Benson's in the cab. Thought maybe you drove it over there and that's why you were gone so long."

"A hat? Oh." A brief flash of red appeared on her face but quickly disappeared. "Yes, I did stop by earlier. I, um, had a tire low on air. The kid's hat must have fallen off."

"It fell off inside the truck?" Wilbur tried to picture how that could have happened.

"I don't know—quit interrogating me, for Christ's sake."

He held his hands up. "All right, all right. I'm sorry. I'll run the truck over tomorrow. Might have a slow leak."

June turned her back on him with a huff. "It's fine. Just forget about it."

Wilbur stared at the back of his wife's head for a moment, waiting for her to cool down. "Hey," he said with a snap of his fingers. "Instead of you cooking tonight, why don't we order pizza? We'll get it from Antonio's. That's your favorite."

"If I say yes, will you go away now?"

His shoulders sagged at the acid-laced question. He turned around and mumbled that he would call in the pizza order in half an hour. With a sigh, Wilbur trudged down the stairs, gripping the banister tightly.

He sat at the kitchen table and heard June's voice from upstairs, clearly back on the phone again. She had that same lilting laugh he remembered from when they were first married. It sounded just like the laugh from his favorite Hollywood movie star, Greer Garson. Closing his eyes, he recalled the jokes and funny stories he used to tell and how his stomach flipped every time she chuckled or giggled with him. Those days seem to be long past now, though. Now she ignored him or, when they did interact, they quarreled. She had gone from Greer Garson to Margaret Hamilton.

It seemed like he could do nothing right anymore. If he did something wrong, she was mad. But if he became cross with her, or questioned her, she became mad. He never had a chance to be angry, always afraid that she would blow up at him, regardless of the situation.

Wilbur had suggested marriage counseling, but she just laughed at him. That had been a couple years ago. Perhaps he should ask again. He sighed, knowing what the outcome would be. "Why bother," he whispered with a slow shake of his head.

"Why bother with what?" June said, standing in the doorway behind him.

Wilbur jumped at the harsh sound of his wife's voice. "Oh, nothing."

"Mm-hmm. Did you order the pizza?"

"Not yet," he said, standing up and reaching for the phone on the wall. "I'll do that now."

She sighed and mumbled something he couldn't make out, but he had dialed and was waiting for Antonio's to pick up, so didn't feel like arguing with her.

"It'll be ready in a half hour. I'll pick it up," he said after hanging up. He shook his head again when she didn't answer.

CHAPTER FOUR

A few minutes later, Wilbur slid into the pickup truck and started the engine. Before he backed up, he leaned down and picked up the Benson's hat lying on the floor. Pursing his lips, he turned it over in his hand, examining it. Not sure what he was looking for, he tossed it on the passenger seat and decided to make a detour before he picked up the pizza.

Driving over the causeway toward town with the windows open and the salt breeze filling the truck, his mind drifted back to some of the talk he had heard in town over the years. He had always ignored it, confident that his wife was always faithful to him. He had given her no reason not to be. They had a good life at the lighthouse. He remembered when they lived in Woburn, just outside Boston. Sure, they were a lot more active then, but that was quite a few years ago. All the parties they went to, or hosted at their house, the dinners and barbeques. June certainly seemed happy then. She had her part time job at the boutique on Newbury Street and her volunteer work, plus her girls' nights out. Their age difference didn't matter to either of them. At least he didn't think so.

When he retired from the Customs Service after thirty years, he recalled vividly sitting June down at the kitchen table and announcing that he wanted to purchase one of the last remaining manned light-houses in the state. It was scheduled to be decommis-sioned in a few years and a new one built, but he wanted to keep tending to it, and turn it into a tourist attraction. He had it all figured out: he would invest much of his retirement into purchasing the light and three-acre plot of land, plus the house. He would maintain it and pocket the profits from tourists.

June didn't seem as enthused about his plan as he did, but he knew she would come around. It was only an hour and a half from their new home to Newbury Street if she wanted to go shopping and two hours to Woburn to visit her friends.

And as he predicted, they both settled into their new life. He had a good retirement from the federal government and June found little things to keep her busy in between her trips into Boston to see her old friends.

They worked together to renovate the small light-house keeper's house, although they argued over the updating she wanted to do. He was fine with repairing what needed fixing, of course, especially as the house was just fifty yards from the ocean. But June wanted to practically tear it down and build a new house. No, no, he recalled telling her. That would never do. It needed to stay in the spirit of the original. We can't have tourists coming to the light-house and seeing a brand-new, modern house right next door. The tour needed to be an authentic experience.

Wilbur had initially wanted to include the house in the tour, but June put her foot down on that idea. Remodeled or original, she wasn't sharing her house with a bunch of strangers, traipsing through it all day. He finally agreed, as long as she agreed to keep it the way it was, except for repairs, of course.

The lighthouse was far enough off the new inter-state that crowds eager to tour it never quite material-ized, a fact that June seemed to enjoy needling Wilbur about. But he didn't mind. There was always some-thing of the old light to fix or clean, and that certainly kept him busy. He wasn't getting rich off it, but with his retirement, they had plenty to live comfortably.

He stopped at the light at Route 3 and glanced over to the hat from Benson's sitting on the passenger seat, then at his watch. He had time to stop by Benson's before the picking up the pizza.

Wilbur's truck rumbled into the Benson parking lot and he pulled to an abrupt stop around the side of the building. The hat slid off the seat and onto the floor. He sighed and unbuckled his seatbelt, leaning over to fetch it.

"Did you forget something, swee—oh, it's you, Wilbur!"

Wilbur sat back up in the truck and turned to face

Max. The man was in his late forties with a tanned face and some light graying around the temples.

"Hello, Max. How have you been?"

"I'm, I'm good, very good, Wilbur. Um, how are you? How's the lighthouse?"

Wilbur wondered if Max had always stammered a bit, but couldn't remember. "She's great. Had a nice family come out for a tour earlier today." He held up the hat. "I think this is yours, or one of the guys," he said, handing it over. "June Bug said she was over here earlier with a low tire and you took care of it."

Max's eyes widened somewhat and his stammer became more pronounced, Wilbur noticed.

"Uh, yeah, front left. This one right here. Might have a, a slow leak. I'm fixin' to close up soon, but we can look at it next week if you want."

"That's fine. No rush. I hadn't even noticed it, so it must be very slow." Wilbur pointed to a cabin cruiser on a boat trailer. "How's the restoration coming?"

"All done, actually. We're—I mean, I'm taking it out in a few days for its shakedown cruise. The new motor has exactly zero hours on it and the hull has an all-new gel coat. And the cabin itself has had a top-to-bottom renovation. I'm excited to take her out."

"Good for you, Max. Well, listen, I'm headed over to pick up a pizza. Have a good night."

"Yup, don't want it getting cold. Bring in the truck next week and I'll look at the tire," he said with a wave as he backed away from the truck.

Wilbur waved goodbye and headed out of the parking lot toward the pizzeria.

CHAPTER FIVE

Wilbur returned home with the pizza, the aroma of a pie topped with sausage, pepperoni, and onions filling the cab on the way back. When he went inside and placed the pizza on the kitchen table, he called to June.

"Honey, I'm home. I got you a treat, too, garlic bread." He was met with silence. "June?" Frowning, he opened the cupboard and retrieved two plates and set them opposite one another on the yellow Formica table. "June?" he called a little louder, heading into the living room to see where his wife was.

He heard the back door open and slam shut. "Did you hear that damned lighthouse?" June yelled. "Ever since you left, it's been making this screeching sound. Something's wrong with it. Of course, it quit the moment you pulled in."

Wilbur paused. "I don't hear anything."

"I just said it stopped. Don't you listen to me at all? Jesus Christ."

He put his hands up to try and calm her. "I'll look at it after dinner. Might be a bearing." He pointed to the table. "I got you your garlic bread."

June sighed heavily and sat at the table, looking blankly at the pizza box. "I'm not even hungry."

Wilbur's shoulders sagged. "At least have a piece of bread."

She reached for the box and flipped it open. "Did you get the marinara sauce?"

"Shoot. I forgot. June Bug, I apologize. I can go back if you want."

"Never mind." She took a bite of the garlic bread and shook her head.

Wilbur ate his pizza in silence, trying to think of something to say to brighten his wife's mood, but he kept coming up blank. When he finished, June was still at the table, staring off into the living room. "I'll wrap this up, dear," he said. "You can have it later or tomorrow."

"Mmm," she replied, standing from the table. "I'm going to bed. See if you can't fix that stupid lighthouse before you come up."

"Gettin' on it right now. I'll calm her down."

"You'll calm her down?" June said, rolling her eyes. "Crazy old fool," she mumbled.

Wilbur frowned as he pulled out the aluminum foil from the drawer and tore off a couple pieces, watching June exit the kitchen and head upstairs. Wrapping the pizza, his nostalgia for the early days of their marriage gave way to melancholy about what was apparently lost forever. But he shook that off as he strode across the grass in the early evening light. He was entering the space that made him forget his wife and her contempt of him.

Opening the lighthouse door, he stood at the base of the great tower, knowing that he was wanted here. Appreciated. Needed. Desired. He placed his palm on the brick wall and felt the rough texture on his fingertips.

He didn't hear any screeching. Instead, the lighthouse spoke to him as it usually did. A whispering moan whirled around him like a ribbon, not quite seen and barely heard. It was a feather tickling the back of his neck and his arms. He stood and breathed deep, filling his lungs with the salt air.

Wilbur closed his eyes and took another breath as the sound rolling through the lighthouse—his lighthouse—grew louder. He could just make out a woman's voice, thin and reedy. It was far away, and he couldn't make out any words, but he knew who it was. Just the sound of her voice filled his heart like music. The more June grew angry with him, the more he retreated to his lighthouse, and the closer he drew toward *her*.

The moaning faded, and he exhaled as the tingly sensation abated. Wilbur opened his eyes and blinked away the sheen of tears that had formed. He started up the stairs to add some grease to the bearings of the motor, running his fingers along the bricks. The gritty texture brought a smile to his wrinkled face.

He smiled, recalling the family that had come earlier. He never told Ed how he knew what had happened all those years ago. The man would think he was a lunatic if he said it was the ghost of the lighthouse that whispered the tale to him. Not in so many words, of course, but he understood enough of the tragedy that occurred almost eighty years prior.

When he opened the door to the power room, he heard a faint scraping from the motor. It was clearly a bearing, but it wasn't loud at all. He had no idea what June was complaining about. *I think she just lives to whine.*

After shutting off the motor, slathering some grease into the bearings, and starting it back up again, Wilbur sighed and sat on the short three-legged stool below the master switch on the wall. With his back against the wall, he felt the vibrations from each turn of the shaft. He leaned his head back and, once his head touched the brick, he could hear her faint voice again.

"Oh, my dear, timing is everything in life, isn't it?" he said out loud. "It's too bad I wasn't around when you were alive. We would have had quite the time, wouldn't we?"

He sat for several long minutes with his eyes closed, leaning back, listening to the hum of the motor and the vibration from each revolution. Opening his eyes, he glanced at the small wooden tool chest mounted on the wall. With his palms firmly on his knees, he heaved himself upward and stood. He pulled open the door to an unused junction box and retrieved a half-empty bottle of bourbon, then headed up the final steps to the platform with the stool under his arm.

Once up on the deck, he sat down facing the water. The wind was brisk and cool, but not cold, and the first sip of bourbon warmed him as it slid down his throat. The sun was behind him, low in the sky, lighting up the clouds on the horizon. As he sat and drank from the small bottle, the color of the sky went from an orange similar to the bourbon that he sipped the last of, to a dull blue. When the stars winked on against the darkening velvet of the night sky, he figured it was time to head down the stairs and into the house.

He retrieved the thick chip of glass from his pocket and stared at it in the fading light. He didn't know what it was, but felt it was connected to the lighthouse somehow. Rubbing his thumb gently over the smooth gilded edge, he swore there was a vibration in it. It was the same vibration that ran through the railing. Wilbur shook his head and put the glass back in his pocket. Too much bourbon tonight.

With a heavy sigh, he rose to his feet. He wobbled a bit and pitched forward, catching himself on the railing, saving himself from a hundred foot fall. He took a few deep breaths and turned away from the rail, and climbed through the hatch to the winding steps below.

Leaning heavily on the wrought-iron railing that spiraled away from him, he took slow, measured steps, careful to not let his body get too far ahead of his feet. The railing gave a little here and there along the way, but he finally arrived at the bottom without incident. He peered into the empty bottle and tilted it forward, letting the few remaining drops melt against his tongue. He would need all the liquid courage he could muster when he walked into the house.

After ambling across the yard, he stumbled up the step and into the kitchen. Just as he started up the stairs to the bedroom, he heard June say goodbye to someone and the sound of the phone being hung up. Wilbur shook his head and half-laughed, half-snorted, then laughed at the noise.

When he reached the doorway to the bedroom, June snapped at him from the bed. "Where the hell have you been all this time? Surely it didn't take you this long to fix your stupid lighthouse."

"She's not stupid. She's mine, and I take care of her," Wilbur said, slurring a couple of the words.

"Oh, you are a fool, aren't you?" she said, rolling over to turn off her light.

"Well, Susannah sure doesn't think so."

June bolted up. "Who's Susannah?" she barked.

"Who's Susannah?" he repeated. "You sure haven't been paying attention these last how many years, have you?" Wilbur sat on the edge of the bed and untied his shoes, glancing over at his wife with a wry smile.

"I've never heard you speak of a Susannah." Her voice was thick and stern. "Someone new in town? So help me—"

"I'll give you a hint. She has long dark hair, porcelain skin, and she's a *much* older woman." Wilbur burst out laughing and laughed even harder when he saw the anger flash across June's face.

June squinted as she rolled back over and switched

off the light, mumbling something that he couldn't quite hear.

Wilbur changed into his pajamas, placing the chipped glass in his drawer of the bureau, and covered it up with some of his old tie clips. He brushed his teeth, watching the white foam dribble from his mouth and join the water spiraling down the drain. When he climbed into bed, he didn't even try to give June her nightly kiss goodnight, figuring neither of them would miss it.

CHAPTER SIX

With the lights off and his eyes closed, Wilbur dozed in and out of sleep, feeling his pulse quicken every 24 seconds, when the beam of light shone through the window. He was quite used to the intruding light and it never disturbed him like it did June. He rather liked it, but never had it touched him in this way before. A ripple of...something...he didn't know what, coursed through his body when the light passed over. It excited him, yet also made him slightly fearful. No, not fear—just nerves at the unfamiliarity of it.

When sleep finally came, after some turning over several times to get comfortable, he was wracked with vivid dreams. Each of them featured frothy gray water, storm clouds overhead, and bright, sudden flashes of gleaming white ripping through the heavy black cloak above. Then the waves faded and the lightning stopped its strobe-like flashing, becoming a soft wash now and then. It wasn't violent like a storm, but calm, and he found himself sitting on the first step of the lighthouse, facing the center, where a slow ribbon of fog was spiraling upward.

Out of the fog he heard a voice, thin and distant at first, but as it grew in volume, a form took shape in the cloudy wisps. Wilbur leaned forward, trying to make out what it was. When he saw it was a woman with dark hair wearing a long, blue, billowing dress, chills raced up his arms. He fought mightily to escape the dream, but couldn't.

"Why are you afraid?" the woman said. "Don't you know me?"

"Are you...?" Wilbur stuttered. "No, it can't be."

"It is," the woman said. "It's been a long time, hasn't it?"

"A long time? What do you mean?"

"I've waited an extremely long time for you. I fear, however, you've not waited for me."

Wilbur looked around, panicked. He knew he was in bed, and could feel himself struggling to wake up, but could not rouse himself.

"Who is she?" the woman in front of him asked. "Have you taken a wife?" The woman seemed to levitate a few inches above the floor while her dress undulated around her.

While she floated, he was frozen in place, straining to wake up.

"Merritt," she said. "I know you can hear me. Why don't you speak?" She leaned forward, but seemed anchored to the spot she hovered over. "Haven't you missed me?"

Wilbur stared at her, transfixed by what he was seeing. Still sure he was dreaming, he was unsure if he could respond, or what he would say. He tried to utter a few syllables, but they were unintelligible, even to him.

"What's that?" the woman said. She twirled around, the folds of her dress billowing upward. "Why don't we dance, Merritt? It's been so long. Remember, we used to dance on the foredeck, watching the moon reflect off the water. Those were magical times, my dear." She extended a hand.

Wilbur shook his head, and with great effort, spoke again. "I'm not Merritt. I'm Wilbur Philpott. Are you... Mrs. Holland? Susannah Holland? Because if so, you clearly have me mistaken for the captain. I've seen pictures of him and we don't look a anything alike."

The woman laughed, first with a suppressed titter, then a quick smile, and finally a full-throated howl that echoed throughout the lighthouse.

"You don't understand, do you?" she asked when she recovered from her laugh. "You *are* Merritt. Captain Merritt Holland. My husband. You carried me to this spot after we ran aground. And it is on this spot that I died in your arms. You tried so hard to save me, but you were spent yourself after dragging me through the surf." She shook her head with a frown. "My valiant captain."

Wilbur leaned back, his eyes wide. "No. How can that be?"

"Wilbur, is it? You truly don't understand, do you? You were born the instant my husband died." She pointed upward at a rope fragment hanging high overhead. "He inhabited your body as you left your mother's womb. The midwife cradled you and handed you to your mother, who named you Wilbur. She couldn't know, of course. But you're my Merritt, through and through."

"What? How can that be? That's, that's not..."

"Possible? I will admit that it does not happen often, but it is not unheard of."

"You're saying I was—what's the word?"

"Don't be afraid to say it. You were reincarnated," she said with a genuine-looking smile.

"But how?"

"I'm not privy to all the machinations of the universe, but I know enough to affirm that you are my husband, albeit in a dramatically different form than what I was used to." A disapproving frown flashed across her face, sizing up decades of inactivity and overeating.

"So, you're...Susannah?"

"Why yes, silly. I thought we had determined that. I am Susannah Holland, in my spirit form, of course, and that's why I'm so glad we're talking now, in this dream of yours. It's taken me years and years to break through your slumber so we can chat. But the moment you snatched the fragment of my witching mirror from the bricks, the connection was established."

Wilbur swung his head from side to side, still not believing what he was seeing or hearing. Susannah's ethereal shape hovered before him. "Your what?"

"When Merritt—when *you*—cradled me in your

arms, I gave you my witching mirror. Its power is unimaginable. With the spells and incantations it can bring forth, you could have done almost anything. Do you remember me telling you to read the *Picatrix*? They were the last words I uttered, but you didn't understand. My soul was slipping away, and I saw you sobbing over me. I watched as you threw the lighthouse keeper out the window. And I stared, helpless, as you tied the rope around your neck and flung yourself from the beam. You held the mirror to your chest, but when the rope pulled taut, you dropped the mirror and it shattered."

Wilbur shook his head in confusion. "I don't understand."

"My essence was almost free, but breaking the mirror trapped me here. The mirror gave me the power to go anywhere, but without it, I've been here for decades. And when you showed up as the new lighthouse keeper, I could hardly believe my good fortune. What are the chances that you, my beloved, would die the instant Wilbur was born? And that you would maintain the light?" The figure twirled around in circles as she grinned, her dark hair and dress spinning outward.

"What do you want with me?" Wilbur ventured.

"What do you think I want? Don't you see? We can be together again."

"We can? How? I don't—"

"So many questions, Merritt. You were never this daft until you inhabited this hulk of a body." She beckoned with an outstretched finger. "Come, I'll show you."

Wilbur hesitated, but then eased himself up from the step. He inched forward, but still maintained a distance of a couple feet from the translucent figure before him.

"Come now, my husband. Do not be afraid. How could I hurt you? You could walk right through me. Without my corporeal body, I'm nothing, just a wisp of fog. Try it!" She pointed at the floor in front of her and whirled her finger behind her. "Walk from here to there, without going around me. No harm will come to you, or me."

"Really?"

"Of course. You can even hold your breath if you like."

Wilbur's hand flew to his mouth, suddenly concerned about something he hadn't considered.

"Please have faith in me," she said. "I would never harm you. Walk through me and you'll see that I speak the truth."

His heart racing, he drew a deep breath and lifted a foot. She nodded when he glanced up at her. He topped off his lungs with another breath and strode across the exact center of the lighthouse, where the ghostly form of Susannah Holland floated.

Wilbur whirled around and stared at her. He patted his chest and arms but felt no different.

She had turned to face him with a smile on her face. "I did not lie to you, my love. You cannot harm me, nor I, you. And why would I? This is what I've been waiting for. For us to be together."

He tilted his head to the side, trying to work out what she was suggesting. "This is a dream. You said so yourself. I can't stay asleep forever. This is no life for us. And you haven't moved from this spot. Are you...stuck?"

"In a very real sense, I am. This is where I died in your arms. The lighthouse is cursed. It was built with bricks from the courthouse in Salem, where nineteen people were tried and convicted in 1692, and later hanged. Once that mirror broke, I became trapped. Stuck, as you say. But now that you're here, there is a way out for me."

"And you say we can be together?" Wilbur's insides flipped at the idea. It was too outrageous, but maybe she was right...

"Oh yes," she blurted. "We can be together for eternity, living the life we had planned for ourselves. One that was cut tragically short so many years ago. Merritt, we were so in love, traveling the world on the seas, you at the helm so proud and heroic." She put her hand to her chest and threw her head back. "We can have that again. Once you're on this side, we can have —and do—anything our heart desires. I want nothing more than to be with you again, Merritt. Please."

Wilbur closed his eyes, a fluttering in his stomach taking hold like never before. Even when he dated June, he never experienced anything like this. He was drawn to her more powerfully than he could have imagined.

"How is any of this possible?" he asked.

"Had this 'Wilbur' not been born the moment you died, we'd be together now. It was only that sorry coincidence that somehow ruined it for us. But now you can rectify that."

Wilbur squinted in confusion. He didn't know what she was driving at, but he would do anything for her now. No one had ever shown such an overwhelming desire to be with him, to share his life. "What do I have to do?"

Susannah looked up and pointed toward the remnant of the noose tied to the crossbeams.

CHAPTER SEVEN

Wilbur woke up with a jolt, sucking in a deep breath. He looked around the room and felt the soft mattress beneath him. Early morning sunlight streamed in through the curtains, warming his already damp forehead. He wiped the back of his hand across it, coming away with a sheen of sweat. His heart rate slowed down as he realized he was safe in bed.

Hearing footsteps, he rolled over to see June coming into the bedroom. He cringed when he noticed she looked less than pleased.

"You kept me up half the night with your tossing and turning and your incessant mumbling."

"What was I saying? Did I talk in my sleep?"

"Are you even going to apologize before you grill me?"

"Of course, June. I'm sorry. I had a heck of a nightmare."

"You must have," she said with a yawn. "I don't think I got more than four hours' sleep."

"I've never had a dream like this. June, this is going to sound crazy, but I think I'm the captain of that ship."

"What ship?"

"The *Yarmouth*. You know, the one that crashed on the rocks at the turn of the century."

"You're not making any sense. Just how much bourbon did you drink?"

"No, it wasn't that. I, I was in the lighthouse, in my dream, and this woman appeared, like a ghost. She *was* a ghost, she even admitted to it. Anyway, she was the wife of Captain Holland. She died in the lighthouse after he pulled her from the ocean. And she told me I was Merritt Holland. That I had been reincarnated."

June laughed out loud then halted, as if to catch him telling a tall tale. Then she rolled her eyes and laughed again. "Wilbur, that is the most preposterous thing I've ever heard. Now you lay off that booze, do you hear me?"

"I swear, it wasn't that. Yes, I had a snootful last night, but this was no dream. I mean, it was, but it felt different. Like no nightmare I've ever had. She was real, June, I tell you." He sat up in bed and rubbed his cheek. "And she wants me to..." His voice trailed off, and he grimaced. Could he do what she asked? Actually kill himself? Living in the afterlife with Susannah had to be better than being with June in this life.

"What? She wants you to what?" June demanded.

He sure couldn't tell her what Susannah wanted

him to do. That much was clear. "Nothing. It's all jumbled up."

"You're the one who's all jumbled up. And I will be, too, 'cause I got no sleep thanks to you."

"I know, June. I said I was sorry. It's not like I could help it. I actually tried to wake up, but I couldn't. It was really quite scary."

"Oh my god, you're a grown man, Wilbur. I swear I'm married to a child." She shook her head and sighed. "Did you at least fix the damned thing so it wouldn't make that horrible sound?"

"Hmm? Oh, I didn't hear anything, but I greased the bearings. It should be fine now."

After breakfast, Wilbur entered the base of the lighthouse and stood just inside the door. He waited for its—her—familiar whispering moan, but the structure was silent. He stared at the spot directly at the center of the floor, where Susannah appeared in his dream, fully expecting her to materialize again in a foggy cloud. Straining to hear anything, he waited for a good ten minutes, but was met with more silence.

A quick movement out of the corner of his eye caught his attention. He gasped, but it was just a dried leaf skittering through the door. While he waited for something—anything—to happen, his mind went back to the dream. Could it be true? he wondered. He didn't know much about reincarnation, past lives, or anything like that. It all seemed so improbable. But being born the same moment the captain died and "inheriting" his soul made sense in a weird sort of way.

Maybe it could be possible. Why else was he drawn to buying this lighthouse when he retired? He had always loved the sea, even as a kid. He recalled going fishing with his dad out on the Cape. They took many trips while he was growing up, either in their small boat close to shore, or the occasional chartered excursion further out, beyond the view of the shore.

Those were the voyages he remembered vividly. In the long periods where nothing was biting, young Wilbur imagined himself piloting his own ship down the Atlantic, past the equator and around Cape Horn to the Pacific. Fighting the wild seas through the Drake Passage at the cape, where winds howled uninterrupted by land, was the maritime equivalent of climbing Mt. Everest, and Wilbur saw himself as the conqueror of the waves.

Wilbur's father, however, had different ideas for his son. A life at sea was hard, dangerous, and too reliant on luck to make a living. Yes, fishing vessels heading out from Gloucester and other New England towns could return from the Grand Banks laden with cod and haddock, and the captain and crew would be richly rewarded, but too often the boat might not make it back at all. Dense fog and rough seas claimed many a ship, Wilbur's father told him, and his mother would never forgive him if he chose such a dangerous job for himself.

"You know how anxious she gets just on our small fishing trips," his father told him more than once.

"Imagine if you were gone for weeks, or months, at a time. You'd put her in an early grave, Wilbur."

Wilbur chose a career with the United States Customs Service, where he worked faithfully for thirty years before retiring. He was always stationed at the Port of Boston, one of the principal ports along the east coast. Inspecting bulk carriers and, later, container ships kept him busy and active. A few promotions landed him in an office overseeing crews of inspectors. Scurrying around the holds of ships in his younger days kept him fit, but riding a desk for the last ten years of his career took its toll.

He was a bit pudgy when he retired, but he knew with just a little exercise, he could get back to his fighting weight. As long as he laid off the sweets. That was sometimes difficult because June knew her way around the kitchen and was an extraordinary baker, whipping up apple pies, lemon meringues, bread puddings, cakes and pastries, and so much more. Maybe when New Year's rolled around, he'd set himself a resolution. Even though no one was around, he sucked in his stomach a bit, sure that he could woo June back once he got back into shape.

Although...another idea crept into his head. He stood taller, tightening his abdomen further. Perhaps Susannah was watching. He might have an easier time of uniting with Susannah than attracting June.

Wilbur sighed, wondering why his lighthouse was quiet this morning. She—or rather, Susannah—was certainly active enough last night in his dream. He shuddered when he recalled his last memory from the dream, pointing upward to where Captain Holland had hanged himself.

He rubbed his whiskers and shook his head. Here he's trying to salvage his marriage, something which all evidence indicates is over, but maybe Susannah is right. If he were to cross over, they could be together. Spirits probably don't have to worry about putting on more pounds, or bad knees, or failing eyesight. A small chuckle escaped his lips. That would be an added benefit.

But...wasn't Susannah a witch? What little research he had done on Captain Holland and his wife when he took over the lighthouse revealed she had been considered one in her hometown of Salem. Could she be trusted?

Wilbur sighed and told himself the whole thing was ridiculous. It was merely a bad dream. None of it was real in the slightest.

The Witch's Point lighthouse stirred as a light breeze blew in from the top window, winding down the stone steps with a plaintive cry. The moan wrapped around Wilbur, seeming not only to whisper to him, but through him. He heard a woman's faint, reedy voice calling his name...but it wasn't Wilbur that he heard. It was Merritt.

The voice came from above him. He looked up and his mouth dropped. It couldn't be. A noose dangling from the crossbeams just wasn't possible.

CHAPTER EIGHT

After Wilbur bolted from the lighthouse, he ran across the small yard as quickly as he could, panting as he went. Once inside the kitchen, he grabbed the dish towel hanging from the handle of the refrigerator and wiped his brow with it. His hands trembled and his knees shook so badly, he was afraid they would knock into each other.

"What's got into you now?" June asked, rolling her eyes. "And don't think about putting that towel back now that your sweat is all over it."

He eased himself down onto a kitchen chair and wiped his face again. "I won't, I promise," he replied absently. Wilbur had always felt like the lighthouse spoke to him, but never so clearly as this. And the noose. He closed his eyes tight, trying to erase the vision of it from his mind.

"Wilbur, you're going to have a heart attack. Now what's the matter?"

For a moment, he wondered if June was toying

with him somehow. Perhaps she had tied the rope there. He shook his head. No, that wasn't possible. But there was only one way to prove it.

"June," he started, his voice shaky. "Would you come out to the lighthouse with me? Just for a moment."

"What in the world for? You know I hate that musty old thing."

"Please."

With a heavy sigh, she crossed the kitchen and opened the door, stepping down onto the grass.

Wilbur followed, but then darted ahead of her. "I'll go first," he said.

"Whatever."

They reached the base of the lighthouse, and Wilbur entered with some hesitation. Once inside, he slowly tilted his head upward, afraid of what he would see.

"So why are we here?" said June, sliding her way past him.

"Because of that—" Wilbur looked at the center of the beams, thirty feet above the floor, his mouth agape. Only the cut rope, the remnants of the noose Captain Holland used on himself, were there. He pointed to it, unable to say anything.

"Yes, I know, the old rope the captain hung himself with. I don't know why you haven't cut it down. It's morbid to keep it there, if you ask me."

"But June. When I was here five minutes ago, it was there. Hanging from the beams. A full noose."

"You're going crazy, Wilbur. I told you to stay off the booze."

He turned and looked her in the eyes. He had to get her to believe it. "I swear it, June. I saw it."

She merely shook her head and gave him a pitiable frown.

Wilbur pointed back at the crossbeams. "It was right there, I tell you. I think she means for me to do what her husband did all those years ago. She says I'm her husband."

He turned back to his wife, but she was already halfway back to the house.

Later in the day, Wilbur met his friend Charlie at the diner for their weekly cup of coffee.

"You're a bundle of nerves, Wilbur. Something the matter? You feeling okay?"

"Nothing more than the usual. No, everything's fine."

"Wilbur, I've known you for over thirty years. I know when everything's fine and when it isn't. Now what's going on?"

Wilbur looked around and lowered his voice. "This is going to sound crazy, but just hear me out, okay?"

Charlie nodded and took a sip of coffee.

"I had this dream last night that—well, frankly, it scared the hell out of me."

His friend leaned in. "Go on."

Wilbur told him everything he remembered from

the dream, and what had happened earlier with the noose. When he finished, Charlie sat back and peered at him over the rim of his glasses.

"I can tell you don't believe me," Wilbur said with a sigh.

"On the contrary, my friend. I think you're telling the truth, and I think I can supply some answers."

"You can?" he asked, sitting upright. But he also knew that his friend could be a bit of a prankster. "Now, Charlie, don't you dare say something like I belong in an asylum," he said with a frown.

Charlie put his hands up. "Not at all. I really believe you. And I believe reincarnation is possible. In fact, I remember reading a book about it from the library a few years ago." He paused, glancing up at the ceiling. "Give me a minute to remember the name."

Wilbur stared at his friend and blinked a few times while he waited. He still wasn't entirely confident that Charlie wasn't messing with him.

Charlie snapped his fingers. "Got it! It's called *The Search for Bridey Murphy*. It's about a woman who underwent something called hypnotic regression. She was taken back through her life to childhood and she remembered everything vividly."

"Really? Interesting."

"Well, here's where it gets pretty wild. The hypnotist keeps taking her back, *before* she was born."

"What, like in the womb?"

"No. Before that. A past life. The woman's name was Ruth something-or-other, living in Colorado, but when she was hypnotized and taken back to before she was born, she said her name was Bridey Murphy. And —get this—she lived in Ireland in the early 1800s. Now this Ruth lady had never been to Ireland and didn't have a trace of an Irish accent. But as Bridey Murphy she did. It was a fascinating book. I think they made a movie about it, too. Anyway, if you say that you used to be the captain of the ship that ran aground near your lighthouse, I don't doubt that for a moment."

Wilbur's eyes grew larger as Charlie told the story. It took him a few moments to process everything he was hearing, but only confirmed what Susannah had told him in the dream.

"Is this book in our library right here, in town?"

"Yeah, that's where I read it."

"I might need to head over there and check it out."

"I think you should," Charlie said. "It's been a few years since I read it, so I might be a little sketchy on the details. But I got the gist of it right."

Wilbur nodded and grabbed a napkin from the holder on the table, withdrawing a pen from his pocket. "What's the name of the book again?"

Charlie told him, and he folded the napkin and stuck it in his wallet.

"If you don't mind, I think I'm going to head over there now," Wilbur said. "Hey, thank you for the information, and for not thinking I'm a lunatic."

"Not at all. You know I like to kid you a lot, but I'm on the level about this."

They left the diner and Wilbur waved to his friend

as he walked to the library. Once inside, he approached the reference desk and pulled out the napkin.

"Hello, Wendy," he said with a smile. "I'm looking for a book called *The Search for Bridey Murphy*," he said to the young woman behind the desk. "I'm not sure who it's by, but I'm pretty sure you have it here."

"Not your usual fare, Wilbur, but let's look. It sounds familiar." The woman rose from her desk and beckoned Wilbur to the card catalog a few yards away. Pulling open a drawer, she thumbed through some beige-colored index cards, pulled one out, and jotted down a number from it on a scrap piece of paper. "Right this way," she said.

Reading mostly Westerns or detective stories, he was in an unfamiliar area of the library now, and glad that Wendy was helping him find the book. This would be a departure for him, that's for sure, but he was certainly curious about what this Bridey Murphy was all about.

The librarian located the book quickly and handed it to him. "Here you are," she said cheerfully. "Are you reading it here, or will you be checking it out?"

"I'd like to check it out, if I can."

"Certainly." She nodded toward the reference desk. "Follow me."

A few moments later, she had stamped the circulation card in the front pocket of the book and handed the book back to Wilbur. He started to leave, but turned back.

"I'd like to see if you have another book, please. I

don't know the exact name, but I think it's called Pick-a-Trick?" he asked, his voice trailing off at the end.

"*Picatrix*?" the woman said, raising her eyebrows.

"Yes, that's it!"

"No," she replied with a chuckle. "I don't think there are too many copies of that. Certainly not something a small-town library will have. I don't think there's even an English translation of it."

"What is it?"

"It's an ancient book of magic and astrology, written in Arabic in the eleventh century. 'Picatrix' is the Latin translation for it. In Arabic, it means The Goal of the Sage. It's essentially a guide for using talismans, which are objects that have magic, or religious, powers ascribed to them. They can heal, or protect, or even harm someone. If you believe in that sort of thing, of course."

Wilbur pursed his lips. He felt a little out of his league and was embarrassed to let her know he had no idea what she was talking about. Still...he had to ask one more question. "These talismans...what would they look like?"

Wendy leaned back in her chair for a moment and her face brightened with an answer. "A rabbit's foot. That's an example of a talisman. People carry them for good luck. It's just a superstition, but I bet lots of people have them just in case."

He nodded. That made sense. His dad always carried a rabbit's foot with him. "Could it be something else, too? Maybe a mirror?"

"Sure," she answered. "Almost anything, big or small, can act as a talisman."

Wilbur reached into his pocket and rubbed the smooth edge of the glass fragment. When he did so, the hair stood up on his arms.

"Is that all?" Wendy asked. She pointed to a nearby display. "We have a new Carter Dickson novel in."

"No, not today." He patted the Bridey Murphy book. "I'm going to give this a try." His mind swirled, trying to make sense of everything he had just learned. He turned and gave the librarian a quick wave, eager to get home.

CHAPTER NINE

Settling into his recliner in the living room as soon as he returned home, Wilbur opened the book with care, bordering on reverence. June had said something about taking the truck into town, but he barely heard her. He devoured the words in the book, eagerly turning the pages, learning how Ruth Simmons underwent what the hypnotist called "age regression", taking her back to her childhood, reliving her school days, who sat in front of her in class, then guiding her to the age of three and a detailed description of her doll and her dog, Buster.

When the hypnotist, and author of the book, Morey Bernstein, described his next step, taking Ruth "over the hump", to a time before she was born, Wilbur's heart beat faster. He held his breath as he turned the pages.

Bernstein tells Simmons she is going to go back until she finds herself in a different time and place. He then describes holding the microphone—as he is recording the session—close to her mouth when he asks what she sees.

"'...scratched the paint off all my bed,'" were the first words spoken by Ruth from that other place and time. Bernstein quizzes Ruth about why she did that.

Wilbur's eyes grew wide as he continued reading.

It turns out that the girl had been spanked by her parents and retreated to her room. Eager to take her revenge on the adult world, she picked the paint off her newly painted bed.

Bernstein then asks the girl her name. "'Bridey... Bridey Murphy.'"

Chills ran up his arms to the back of his neck as he realized what he was reading. Somehow, Bridey Murphy had been reincarnated as Ruth Simmons.

He read the next chapter about how Bernstein went from hypnosis skeptic to believer, and a student and practitioner of it. He read all he could on it and even cured his wife of her persistent headaches. Bernstein cured a young man of persistent stuttering, another with insomnia, others with smoking and other habits they were trying to quit.

Wilbur grew more and more fascinated by how hypnosis had helped so many people. He didn't know it could be used in such a fashion. He thought it was only for entertainment; making spectators at a show walk around the stage like a chicken or bark like a dog or whatnot. But there was actual power in hypnosis.

It was the chapters in the book that dealt with age regression that really interested him, though. It all sounded so fantastic, but what other explanation was there? Ruth Simmons had never been to Ireland in her life, and here she was speaking with a thick Irish accent describing her childhood living in Cork, starting when she was eight. She was the daughter of a barrister, Duncan Murphy, and his wife, Kathleen, and they lived in a house called The Meadows. She eventually married Sean McCarthy, a barrister himself, who taught at Queen's University in Belfast, to which she moved.

More bizarre, Bridey told Bernstein that she had died in 1864 from a fall and watched her own funeral and even described her gravestone. Almost sixty years later, she was "reborn" as Ruth Simmons, but she didn't know exactly how.

Wilbur was impressed with the rich detail that Bridey recounted in telling the tale over several hypnosis sessions. And with every page, he grew more and more convinced that he was the reincarnated captain.

Skimming over some of the later chapters that discuss hypnosis in general, he finished the book that afternoon. Goosebumps rose on his arms as he realized what he must now do. He went to the kitchen and reached under the small table that sat below the wall phone.

June had returned by this point, although Wilbur had barely remembered her coming in the house. He knelt down and was sorting through the books and papers on the shelf.

"What are you looking for?" his wife asked, sitting at the kitchen table.

"The phone book."

"Who are you calling?"

"Nobody. Do you know what happened to it?"

"Nobody? You're obviously calling somebody if you're looking for the phone book. Who is it?"

Wilbur sighed. "You'll just make fun of me."

She chuckled, and her voice softened. "I won't. I promise."

"Well, I just read this book about past lives and reincarnation. There was this woman—"

"Reincarnation?"

"Yes, just hear me out." When she nodded, he continued. "I was at the diner with Charlie earlier and I told him about my dream. When I was done, he said he read a book about a hypnotist who had a patient that he put in a trance and took her back to before her childhood. Turns out she was a child living in Ireland decades before the woman was alive. In the book, the author talks a lot about this age regression thing that can be done with hypnosis, and I'd like to try it."

"Try what? Hypnosis?"

"Yeah. I'd like to go under, as it's called, and have the person take me back to before my childhood. If I talk about being at sea and that my name is Merritt Holland, then I'll know it's true. That it's not just in my head or a dream."

June sat, twisted around in the kitchen chair, staring at him. Wilbur wasn't sure what to make of her expression.

"Any chance Charlie is pulling your leg? He's done it before, you know."

Wilbur shook his head. "No, I know he has, but not this time. He was serious—told me the name of the book and everything." Wilbur gestured to the living room. "That's what I've been doing all afternoon, reading it. It's *The Search for Bridey Murphy*. Maybe you'd like to read it."

June's stare turned to a polite smile as she shook her head no. "So you need the phone book to do what, exactly?"

"I want to look up a hypnotist. There's probably none in town, but closer to Boston, there probably is."

She sighed and, with a grand gesture, pointed to the stacks of papers and envelopes on the table in front of her. "Here you go, captain," she said as she handed him the phone book.

Wilbur took the phone book from her but studied what was spread out on the table. "What's all this?" He leaned over and saw that one of the large envelopes was labeled *Wills*. "What are you doing with this?"

June turned back and gathered up the papers. "Nothing. Just making sure everything is up to date."

"Up to date? What's changed? We don't have any kids or anything."

"It's a good idea to check your wills, that's all," she retorted. "I saw a commercial about it on TV the other day."

Wilbur nodded with a frown and sat at the table, thumbing open the phone directory. He watched as she stuffed the papers back into the manila envelope and left the room. Taking a deep breath, he flipped the pages until he came to listings for hypnotists. As he suspected, he couldn't find any in town, but there was one in a suburb of Boston about a half hour away.

It surprised him that his hands were shaking as he stood to dial the phone. Nothing to be nervous about, he told himself. When the line picked up, he didn't know quite what to say. He realized he should have rehearsed the call before he dialed, so he slammed the receiver onto the hook, ending the call more abruptly than he had wanted.

Sitting back down, Wilbur took several deep breaths and ran through what he should say when he called back. After several minutes, he felt calm enough to try again. He didn't think he should just blurt out that he was a reincarnated ship's captain, so when the receptionist answered again, he told her he wanted to make an appointment with the hypnotist to help him remember something important that had happened to him in his childhood.

The receptionist took his information and scheduled him for that Thursday, two days from now, at ten o'clock. Wilbur dutifully wrote down the date and time and thanked the woman, setting the phone down gently after he said goodbye.

His nerves returned, but now it was excitement that coursed through Wilbur. He was going to receive confirmation that not only was he the ship's captain, but—and this was even more important—that Susannah was real and could be trusted.

CHAPTER TEN

The next morning, Wilbur rose early, excited that he was a day closer to his appointment with the hypnotherapist. He wanted to keep tomorrow clear, so decided to head into town to the hardware store to get some parts for the lighthouse. Thursday was usually his day for basic maintenance on the motor, but he moved it to today, and found he could barely concentrate on what he needed while he was perusing the aisles of nuts and bolts, bearings, bushings, and other parts.

Not only was he looking forward to the age regression and what it would reveal, but a small part of him was eager to prove to June that he wasn't crazy. She'd have to believe him after a couple of sessions with the hypnotist.

He made small talk with the young man behind the counter as he made his purchases, not fully paying attention. The clerk had said something about the weatherman predicting a dangerous storm around this time next week, but Wilbur didn't catch all the details.

He puttered around town a while longer, dropping off some brochures for the lighthouse at the motel by the interstate and then to the nursery for some flowers. He liked to have flowers around the lighthouse, even though the salt spray from the ocean meant he had to replace them often. Wilbur thought about getting some flowers special for June but decided against it. She didn't really appreciate those kinds of gestures anymore, and it would just make him sad.

Once he arrived back home, he unloaded the plants in the yard and dropped the brown paper bag with the small parts just inside the lighthouse door. "Better tell June Bug I'm home," he said to himself as he headed across the yard.

"Hi, sweetheart," he called, ducking his head into the kitchen. "I'm heading to the light to give her a thorough cleaning and work on the motor to make sure it doesn't make any noise for you."

"All right," came her distant and bored response from the living room.

He retrieved his toolbox from the hall closet and strode back across the lawn. There was only a slight breeze today, so the lighthouse was quiet as Wilbur climbed the steps to the top. He gripped the handrail, however, and felt the reassuring hum in the metal. Susannah was watching him, he thought with a smile.

His first step once he got to the top was to flip off the main circuit breaker to the light and motor. He stepped into the chamber that held the motor and unscrewed the panel that exposed the wiring. Salt got into everything here, and he wanted to check that first. He laid the curved metal lid on the floor next to him, placing the four screws inside it, and replaced the Phillips head screwdriver back in the box. Wilbur recalled his father teaching him to be careful and deliberate with his tools when working on any job. Keeping parts together and tools where they belong meant doing a thorough, safe job and not losing tools.

Which made it even more strange when he noticed that a small adjustable wrench was missing. He paused to remember when he had used it last, and why he wouldn't have returned it. Wilbur frowned, trying to solve the slight mystery, then recalled adjusting one of the feet on the washing machine. That must have been it, but why wouldn't he have—

An unfamiliar noise from below interrupted his thoughts. It sounded metallic, but he couldn't be sure. For a fleeting moment, he wondered if it was Susannah, but it didn't sound like her windy moans or her thin voice in his dream. The wind picked up at that point and he heard it whistling through the lighthouse. With a shrug, he returned to the electrical panel in front of him.

Aiming his flashlight onto the board, he inspected the connections and saw one that was showing some rust, so he unscrewed the wire and replaced the screw. He found a couple others that needed replacing and wondered if, at some point, the whole motor assembly would have to be taken apart. Wilbur wondered if that was a job he could take on or if it would require a specialist of some sort. Probably something to think about before long. Taking care of his investment was important and preventative maintenance was key. June would object, of course, because of the cost, but this was his baby. And, more importantly now, the glorious structure that had become his obsession housed—as bizarre as it was to say—his first wife. His true wife. June didn't love him anyway, he knew. But Susannah! Theirs was a love for the ages.

Wilbur finished inspecting the panel and other elements of the motor, replacing small parts here and there. He wiped down the glass, added some more grease to the bearings so they'd stay extra quiet, and locked everything up tight.

Making his way down the stone steps, he leaned heavily on the iron railing. The trip up was always easier than heading back down. He could make it to the first landing without holding onto the railing, but going down, he needed to be more careful where he placed his feet. His knees just weren't like they used to be and he relied on the handhold to descend safely.

Wilbur was a third of the way down when the railing gave way.

One leg pitched out in front of him, the other folded up underneath. He scrambled instinctively as he bounced down several steps on his backside, the toolbox flinging out ahead of him.

He yelled in pain and shock and finally arrested his fall after bumping down several steps when his foot caught and his right hand gripped the railing.

Wilbur sat on the step, panting, still in shock. He

rose a bit and stretched out his other leg. Nothing seemed broken and, surprisingly, he wasn't in pain. He knew it was the adrenaline and when it faded, he would be more than sore, in several places. There were already some reddish bruises forming under the skin on his arms.

Still sitting, he looked up at the handrail and tugged on it. It was held fast to the wall all the way down, but above him it was loose. After a few more minutes to catch his breath, he carefully stood, not wanting to put too much weight on the railing. Once he was fully upright, he flexed both legs, making sure he had full movement in them. The one that had crumpled beneath him was already feeling quite sore, but he was confident he could still walk on it.

He took a couple steps up and examined the railing. The bolts that secured it to the wall were missing. He counted seven empty holes in the railing where the bolts should be. Very strange. He wondered how long those had been missing. Maybe one had been gone for a while, which didn't affect anything, but over time the others worked themselves loose. He would have to be more vigilant in checking the bolts, he said to himself. Make it part of his maintenance routine more frequently.

Turning back around, he stepped gingerly down the stairs, trying to keep only minimal weight on the rail. The toolbox had made such a racket tumbling down that he expected it to have burst open and his tools scattered along the stairs, but as he neared the bottom, he was pleased to see it intact near the entryway.

The closer he got to the bottom, the easier he breathed. And it was around that time that he heard Susannah's whispers swirling around him, obviously concerned about him.

"I'm okay, dear," he said. "It was a bit of a scare for me. And for you, too, I'm sure. But I'm fine."

When he reached the bottom, he noticed seven metal bolts resting on the floor, all together in a haphazard pile.

"What in the world?" he murmured, running a hand against his cheek.

CHAPTER ELEVEN

Wilbur trudged across the yard carrying his toolbox, and opened the back door.

June was at the table and shot a startled look at him, her eyes wide. "Wilbur!"

"Yeah, I guess I look a mess, don't I?"

"No. I don't think—what do you mean?" June's voice was a little higher in pitch than normal.

"Well, I almost fell down the stairs."

"I've told you to lay off that bourbon," she said, her face and tone more relaxed now.

Wilbur shook his head. "It wasn't that at all." He stretched out his arm and flexed his legs again. "The railing pulled away from the wall. If I had been leaning forward, I probably would have somersaulted down the whole way. Probably would have died. Instead, I ended up on my keister and only slid a few steps. I'm going to be sore tomorrow, that's for sure. And the damnest thing was, the bolts were at the bottom of the steps. You would think they'd be strewn all over the stairs. And on top of all that, I can't find my monkey wrench. The small one. You haven't seen it, have you?"

June frowned and shook her head. "I never touch your tools, Wilbur. I'd be too afraid of not putting one back in just the right spot." She shook a finger at him. "That stupid lighthouse is going to be the death of you yet."

Wilbur straightened at the comment, the butterflies taking flight again at the prospect of being with Susannah. "Actually, I think it's going to be my salvation," he whispered.

"What was that?"

"Nothing," he said with a sigh.

June twisted around in her chair as he walked into the living room. "You're up to something, I can tell. Are you still thinking you're the damned captain?"

He said nothing in response, but kept walking until he reached his recliner. Easing himself down, he extended the footrest and grabbed the latest *Ellery Queen's Mystery Magazine* from the end table. He could feel his muscles tightening up and breathed heavily, not looking forward to the inevitable pain and stiffness that was to come.

Wilbur rested his head back and closed his eyes, listening to the crashing surf in the distance. The shock and adrenaline had worn off, and he drifted off to sleep.

When he woke up, it was almost dark. Wilbur glanced at his watch and saw that it was a little past seven. "June," he called, looking around but not seeing her. "June!"

"Yes, dear," she said, coming down the steps from the second floor. Her voice was heavy, dripping with insincerity.

"How long did I sleep? How come you didn't wake me?"

She threw her hands up. "I don't know. I went into town and got something for dinner, got back a little while ago. Why is it up to me to make sure you're up?"

"Are you going to make dinner?"

"Yes, I was just about to start. Why don't you...go do something, I don't know."

Wilbur reached over to the lever and brought the footrest down. "I probably should get those bolts screwed back in. Can you imagine if a tourist fell?"

"God forbid. We'd probably have to shut down the biggest tourist attraction on the east coast," she said with a sarcastic laugh.

He didn't have the energy to respond, but went to the kitchen and left out the back door with his tool chest. With a groan, he bent over and scooped up the bolts from the floor of the lighthouse, and cautiously made his way up the stone steps.

When he reached the point where the bolts were missing, he set the toolbox down and opened it. The large adjustable wrench should work, he thought. He peered in and moved some other tools aside to look for it when he spotted the small wrench.

"Now how can that be?" he said. He looked around. "Susannah? Is this your doing? I'm positive the wrench wasn't here earlier."

This time, no wind picked up in response. The air was still, and he heard nothing as he tightened the bolts, securing the railing against the bricks.

He returned to the house just as June was serving herself a plate of pot roast with potatoes and carrots.

"Is there enough for me?" Wilbur asked.

"Of course. But I didn't know how long you'd be out there and I was hungry. Here, take this," she said, handing him the dish. "I'll make another plate."

They ate in relative silence, which had become the norm lately. Wilbur felt the soreness coming on strong and, even though he had taken a long nap in the afternoon, he knew he'd be going to bed soon.

He reached for a piece of bread and winced in pain.

"I'll get it," June said with a sigh, spreading a pat of butter on it and handing it to him.

After a few moments, she spoke again. "Why don't you take a bath before you go to bed? And pour in some Epsom salt. It'll help with the soreness."

"Thank you, dear. I'll do that."

Once the dishes were done, he headed upstairs for his bath. June surprised him by following him and drawing the bath for him, pouring in a generous amount of the salt while he got undressed. The water provided a welcome relief to his tightening muscles, and he spent a long time with his head resting against the back wall of the bathroom, just letting the warmth penetrate his aching body.

When he finished, he dried off and changed into his pajamas. June had gone downstairs, probably watching TV. He was just about to get into bed when he remembered his magazine. Yes, that will be just the thing to help him fall asleep.

Wilbur padded quietly down the steps to the living room, which was empty. Just as he wondered where she could be, he heard her speaking softly in the kitchen. It was after nine o'clock and he pondered who she could be talking to. He approached the kitchen and as he drew within earshot, he heard her say, "...it didn't work. I don't know what I'll do now."

He turned the corner and saw that she was on the phone.

She whipped her head around to face him and then spoke again to the receiver. "Good to talk to you, Carol. I'll see you later." She turned back to Wilbur. "I thought you were in bed."

"I finished my bath and realized I had forgotten my magazine. Was that Carol Ferguson?"

"Hmm? Yes, Carol. I haven't seen her in a while and she was catching me up on everything."

Wilbur nodded his head and stood in the doorway, just looking at her, unsure if she was telling the truth. He considered asking her what didn't work, but he was too tired to get into another argument.

"You have your appointment tomorrow with that hypnotist, right?" she asked.

"Yes, um, ten o'clock."

"You want to be well-rested for that, I expect, so..."

"All right then. I should probably head up. Are you coming to bed soon?"

"About another half hour," she replied. "Run along now. I'm going to tidy up in here a bit. And don't forget your magazine."

He scanned the spotless kitchen, wondering what needed to be cleaned up, but again decided not to pursue the matter.

"Good night, June," he said as he turned to leave.

CHAPTER TWELVE

Although he was in a fair bit of pain from his bumpy trip down the steps in the lighthouse, Wilbur slept pretty well, especially for being keyed up about his visit to the hypnotherapist. He was hoping for another dream featuring Susannah, but they were just run-of-the-mill dreams, nothing of any significance. Waking up, he stretched and discovered that, as he feared, he was much sorer today than yesterday.

He rose from the bed gingerly, easing himself down to the floor and standing up gently, not wanting to further injure himself. Everything seemed in working order, so he began his morning rituals, glad that he had woken up a little earlier since he'd have to take things slowly for the next few days.

He had to temper his excitement about his appointment this morning as he got ready. "I feel like a kid at Christmas," he told June when he came downstairs and sat at the kitchen table.

His wife was quiet, and shook her head slowly. "What time is your appointment?" she asked as she put a plate of scrambled eggs in front of him. "I'd like to go into town, do some shopping, early afternoon."

"Oh, that shouldn't be a problem, June Bug," he said. "Er, sorry—June," he corrected himself. "My appointment is at ten, remember? I think it goes for an hour. So I should be back by eleven-thirty at the latest."

"Good. Now, tell me again who you're going to see. And what are they doing to you?"

"Dr. Beckett. He's going to put me in a trance and take me back to my childhood and then *before* my childhood. Before I was born."

"When you were the captain?"

"Yes!" Wilbur nodded before picking up his fork.

"I see. Well, okay," she said with a shrug.

He waved his finger at her. "I know you're skeptical, but I have confidence in this doctor. I mean, I know a lot of the story behind the captain, but he'll be able to fill in the details, I'm sure."

"All right. Have fun. And don't be late coming back."

"I won't." Wilbur finished his eggs and had a cup of coffee before he finished getting ready.

Wilbur was in the tail end of the morning rush hour heading into Boston, but fortunately got off the highway before it became too congested. Referring to the scrap of paper with the address a few times, and making a wrong turn, he finally found the small office complex where the doctor's office was.

Once inside the building and walking down the hallway, he realized how nervous he felt. Standing outside the office door, he took a deep breath and smoothed out his shirt. With a final quick breath, he turned the knob and entered.

It was a nondescript medical waiting room, like most others. The woman behind the desk greeted him and asked him to sign in and take a seat. There were a few other people in the room, and he figured that there must be more than one doctor for the office. His assumptions were confirmed when he saw the four photographs on the wall, with names below them, Dr. Beckett being one of them.

He only had to wait a few minutes when the receptionist called him forward. Once inside Dr. Beckett's office, the middle-aged man introduced himself and shook his hand. The doctor had a crewcut and black-rimmed glasses, and a friendly smile.

"I understand you'd like to undergo age regression hypnosis. Is that right?" Dr. Beckett said, sitting down in a wingback leather chair and gesturing to a matching one.

Wilbur stuttered a bit, but found his voice. "Yes, yes, I think I'd like to try it."

"May I ask why? Have you suffered some trauma, or is there something disturbing you? Something you'd like to explore? Hypnosis is just one therapy; there are other treatment types depending on what exactly is troubling you."

"No, I definitely want to be taken back."

"Taken back to your childhood?" Beckett asked, turning his head a bit, but keeping his eyes locked on Wilbur.

"Well..." Wilbur started to speak, but his voice trailed off.

The doctor looked at his notes. "Mr. Philpott, before we go too far, I think it's best that you tell me exactly why you're here. Usually a patient has some issue they're trying to get relief from, or a habit they're trying to break, something like that." He looked at his pad again. "I don't really have any information on you, so I can't make any recommendations."

Although he was afraid the doctor would think he was a lunatic, Wilbur decided he needed to tell him everything. He knew he only had an hour, so he tried to condense it as much as possible. Looking at the clock, he saw that he still had forty minutes left in the session when he was finished. He hoped it was enough. "So... what do you think, Doctor?"

"Well, that's quite the tale, Mr. Philpott." The man leaned back in his chair with his eyes wide and his mouth hanging slightly open.

"You don't believe me?" Wilbur asked, his shoulders sagging.

"On the contrary. I've done a lot of research in age regression and past lives. I think there's definitely something to the whole phenomenon. What is striking about your account is the vividness of it and your recall, without even being under hypnosis. And, if I'm being honest, the drama of the story. Most patients in the literature that I've studied lead pretty normal lives, both in the present and in their past life. But a ship's captain, sailing the high seas, surviving a shipwreck, that's Errol Flynn stuff right there."

Wilbur chuckled at the comparison, but it pleased him that he had impressed the doctor with what he had experienced. He glanced at the clock again. "Doctor, I know we only have an hour and I'd love to be taken back. I'm not sure how long the procedure takes."

Beckett looked at his watch. "We have plenty of time. Would you like to get started?"

"Yes, please! What do I need to do?"

"You can sit there if you're comfortable." He gestured toward the sofa. "Many people feel more relaxed there, however. It's typically easier to fall into a trance if you're relaxed."

Wilbur stood and crossed to the couch. "Yes, this will be better," he said, stretching out. "Do you dangle a watch in front of me or something?"

Dr. Beckett laughed. "No, no. Nothing like that. But I will have you focus on that point on the wall." He pointed along Wilbur's line of sight. "See that star? That's what I want you to look at."

On an otherwise blank wall, the small, brass, many-pointed star was easy to spot. "So, just look at the star? That's all I have to do?"

"That, and concentrate on my voice and my words. Now, at no time will you be asleep or unconscious. You will be very relaxed, so just continue to listen to my voice. Keep gazing at the star on the wall as you focus on my voice. Close your eyes. You can probably feel yourself relaxing now. You're letting yourself slip deeper and deeper into a calm, peaceful state. As I continue to talk, you'll feel yourself sinking deeper into that relaxed state. As you listen to my voice, I want you to imagine yourself on a staircase in a warm, quiet room. You're at the top of the stairs, but take a step down, nice and easy, and another step. With each step, you'll feel yourself floating blissfully away in a calm, serene state of utter relaxation. You have several more steps to go and at the bottom, you'll notice a closed door. As you sink further into relaxation with each step, you approach the door. When you're ready for pure relaxation, open the door and step through."

Wilbur's eyes had closed, and he felt his muscles relax and all the tension vanish from his body. He pictured the door in his mind's eye, just like the doctor said, and he opened the door, walking through it. Serenity and peace surrounded him. He was no longer aware of anything in the room. It was like floating on a cloud. He couldn't hear anything except the doctor's soothing voice.

"Are you through the door, Wilbur?" Dr. Beckett asked.

"Yes," he murmured.

"Very good. As we progress, we're going to walk down further staircases. But right now, I want you to focus on how peaceful you feel, how at rest you are. Think of it as standing on a landing for now. When you're ready, we'll go down a few more steps to the next door, and the next landing. For now, just breathe quietly, in and out. Concentrate on your breathing, feel your chest rise and fall with each breath. Are you ready to take some more steps?"

Wilbur nodded his head slightly. "Yes."

"Excellent. Take a step down, then another. With each step, we're going to go back in time a little. When you take a step, I want you to recede in time by five or ten years. After you take a step, tell me what you see."

After a pause, Wilbur saw himself taking a step down a flight of stairs. He was younger now, puttering around the lighthouse. "I'm inside the lighthouse," he said. "I'm heading up the top, replacing some rusty hinges on the door that takes you out to the platform."

"Is it a sunny day, or cloudy, windy, rainy? Warm or cold?"

"It's a nice day, just a small breeze coming off the ocean. There's a fishing boat headed out for the evening."

"Take another step, Wilbur. Go back ten more years and tell me where you are and what you're doing."

"I'm in the office wrapping up some paperwork. We intercepted some containers of counterfeit goods from China. Designer stuff. Purses, things like that. I thought of grabbing one for June," he said with a chuckle.

"Very good, Wilbur. You're doing great. Let's take a few more steps. Take me back twenty years. What do you see?"

"I'm at Fenway, watching the Red Sox and Indians.

Cleveland lost yesterday but is proving they're not a pushover today. They've struck out Joe Harris each time he's come to the plate. I might leave in the seventh to beat the crowd, catch a beer across the street, and take the T home."

"How old are you, Wilbur?"

"Uh, twenty-five."

"And you work for..."

"US Customs. Just got on with them."

"So it's what year, nineteen...?"

"Nineteen twenty-three."

"And you're not married to June yet, are you?"

A flash of confusion crossed Wilbur's face. "June? Who's...? Oh, June. No, not yet. I haven't met her yet. That won't be for a while."

"Okay, go on," Dr. Beckett said.

"Me and the boys try to catch a couple baseball games each month. Billy and me, mostly. Neither one of us is married, and we'll go after work, or on a Saturday. They're playing pretty lousy this year, and definitely won't come anywhere close to the Yankees."

"Let's take a couple more steps down that staircase, all right? How about another twenty years back? When you get to the bottom of the steps, there will be another door. Step through it and tell me what you see at five years old."

Wilbur murmured a bit as he saw himself descending the stairs, opening the door, and walking through it. It was like gazing through fog, but it cleared the longer he stayed on the landing, looking around.

"What do you see, Wilbur?"

He shivers a bit and gathers up his shirt around his collar. "It's cold. I can see my breath. Dad and I are climbing back up the hill with the sled. Once we get to the top, he said we'll go down one more time and then go back in for hot chocolate."

"Sounds like fun. Take me inside your house. Tell me what's in your bedroom."

Wilbur opened the door to his bedroom in his mind and stepped inside. He picked up the baseball mitt from his dresser and breathed in the leather scent. Seeing his bed with the boat and anchor pattern on the bedspread filled him with nostalgia. Red Sox pennants adorned the wall above his bed. He returned the baseball glove to the dresser, placing it next to a wooden model of a tall sailing ship. A small desk painted blue sat below the window, with an empty tin can full of pencils and crayons.

"You like your room, Wilbur?"

"Very much."

"What do you see in it?"

Wilbur described everything he set his eyes on, smiling at the sight of the glove, the pennants, the bedspread, the ship model.

"Tell me about that ship," the doctor said.

"Dad brought it back for me from one of his trips," he said, his voice slow, trying to stretch out and savor the warm feelings that bubbled up inside him.

"Did you assemble it?"

"I helped him put it together. Dad said I did such a good job with it I could be a shipbuilder. I told him I wanted to be a ship's captain instead."

"I see," Beckett said, his voice steady and even. "Let's take another step down, and then another. I want you to tell me the earliest thing you can remember."

Wilbur took another couple steps. His memory was hazy, but he had flashes of recall. Birthday parties, balloons, presents, cake. Falling off the swing in the backyard and hurting his arm. Getting into a fight with a neighbor boy. Finding a dead bird in the gutter, swarming with maggots. These memories came out in a halting voice as he strained to remember.

"Can you go back further for me, Wilbur?"

"I can't breathe. It's dark but getting lighter. Now I'm crying. I hear voices around me. Other sounds. I don't know where I am."

"Very good. You're safe, Wilbur," the doctor said, his voice rich and reassuring. "There's a door in front of you at the bottom of this flight of stairs you just walked down. When you open it, you'll be in a different place, a different time. A *before* time. I want you to twist the knob and open the door. Tell me when you've done that."

Wilbur pushed open the door and stood, gazing out at a pure white fog. "It's all cloudy. I can't see anything."

"That's okay. You're perfectly safe. I'm here with you. Walk through the door and tell me where you are."

Wilbur stepped over the threshold. The door vanished behind him. He was surrounded by a swirling, colorless cloud. His body swayed slightly.

Cold sweat beads formed on his forehead while the fog cleared. Once his vision cleared, he spoke in a fevered, frightened voice. "I hear men shouting. The ship is bucking and heaving with the waves. I'm fighting the wheel to hold it steady, steering it into the waves. Rain is driving sideways. Other than the distant lights on the shore and the running lights of the ship, it's pitch black. My first officer runs past me to the hold, trying to rescue the men below. He turns to look at me before he climbs down and I see his face in the glow of the lanterns—he's a dead man. I know I'll never see him again.

"I feel the wheel go slack in my hands. The rudder has broken. We're doomed now. The ship is thrown sideways and a wave slams into us, catching us broadside. We keel over almost to the point of capsizing, but she rights herself as we pitch down the back of the wave into the trough. The next wave picks us up and smashes us against the rocks. The hull splinters and men shout and scream as the boat is swamped with more waves.

"Then I hear it, an ear-piercing shriek that pierces the night, louder than the waves and the men. Susannah!"

CHAPTER THIRTEEN

Wilbur's eyes flung open and he twisted his head around, trying to get his bearings. Susannah's cries echoed in his mind and his heart, but all he heard was a man's voice.

"Wilbur, are you okay? You're safe. Tell me what you saw," Dr. Beckett said.

He caught his breath and forced himself to calm down. When he blinked, he saw the whitecaps from the storm and his body swayed from the ship slamming into the rocks. Closing his eyes, he saw Susannah. Taking his time, not wanting to come back to the present, he reached out to her.

"Wilbur?" the doctor repeated, touching his arm.

He glanced at the doctor, still a bit confused, but settled himself, realizing he was still on the couch in the hypnotherapist's office.

"Where were you?"

"I was on a ship—my ship. It was the *Yarmouth*, sailing from Halifax. It was night, but I could see lights in the distance. And a terrible storm." He paused to catch his breath. "We hit a shoal, men were screaming belowdecks. The hull had breached. Water must have been flooding in. They were trapped and then, then I heard my...wife." He blinked back tears at the thought of Susannah in danger. "It was her, Doctor. Susannah. She was crying. In our quarters. She was trying to get out, but the door was jammed. She kept shouting my name—Merritt." He gazed at the doctor. "That's when I woke up, or came to, or whatever."

Beckett tapped his pen against the notebook and pursed his lips. "This shipwreck...it was what you described to me at the beginning, right?"

Wilbur frowned. "Yes. Are you saying you don't believe me? It's all in my head? I mean, didn't you take me back to before I was born?"

"Well, it's not that I don't believe you. I'm sure you had a very visceral experience just now. I could sense it just watching you. You were sweating and in a bit of discomfort, I could see. If you hadn't come out of the trance, I was about to bring you out of it."

"But that's not the same as you believing that I experienced a past life, that I'm Captain Holland."

"Mr. Philpott, in cases such as these—"

"What do you mean by 'cases such as these'?" he interrupted, growing angry.

"The fact is that you came to me specifically for age regression therapy. Usually, the patient comes with a complaint of some sort. Something they can't let go of, some deep-rooted problem. And one of the available therapies is age regression, to see if there is some underlying cause from childhood. I don't use it all the time. I probably only use it in about a tenth of my cases. Many patients don't even know the treatment exists. But you came to me, seeking it out. You not only knew about it, you had actively studied it by reading about the Bridey Murphy case." Beckett leaned forward a little in his chair. "Being on that ship was the outcome you wanted from the start. You even described a model ship being on your dresser as a child. Now you may indeed have had one, but there's also a good chance you didn't. The mind is a very tricky thing, Mr. Philpott."

"But I remember that wooden ship. I can see it on my dresser plain as day."

"I'm sure you can. And, again, if we could get in a time machine and go back to your room at six years old, chances are good that it would be there. But your mind could also have filled in the gaps over the last sixty-some years and put that ship there on your dresser."

Wilbur shook his head, firmly believing that he had a ship in his room as a young boy. He started to speak, but the doctor interrupted.

"Let's try a brief experiment. I'm going to give you a list of words. And then we'll talk some more. Are you ready?"

Wilbur wasn't sure where he was going with this, but he nodded in agreement.

"Okay. Here we go: Soda, heart, tooth, tart, taste, bitter, good, sugar, candy, nice, chocolate, pie, sour, and cake."

After a pause, Wilbur said, "Is that it?"

"For now, yes." Beckett leaned back in his chair. "I would like you to come back on Tuesday, if you could. I'd like to explore this past life of yours a little further, before the shipwreck, if that's all right."

"So you do believe me?" Wilbur was hopeful once again that the doctor took him seriously and could provide answers.

"I never said I didn't. But after one session, I have little to go on. I'd like to do a few more."

"Fair enough, Doctor. Yes, I can be here on Tuesday."

"Very well. You can schedule it with the receptionist."

Wilbur rose from the couch and turned to the door.

"Before you go, Mr. Philpott. A few moments ago, I had given you a list of words. Do you remember?"

"Oh, yes, of course." He turned back to face Beckett.

"Do you recall if I said the word 'pie'?"

"Yes, you did."

"And how about 'tart'?"

Wilbur nodded. "Mm-hmm."

"Very good. And how about 'sugar'?"

"Sugar? Yes."

"Did I say the word 'honey'?"

"Honey? Um, no, I don't believe so."

"Good. Did I say 'sweet'?"

"Yes," Wilbur affirmed with a nod.

"Are you sure?" Beckett asked with a turn of his head.

"Sweet? Yes, definitely."

The doctor drew a breath. "I'm afraid your memory is faulty, Mr. Philpott. I did not say 'sweet'."

"I could have sworn you did," Wilbur said, twisting his face in confusion.

"And now you see how just how malleable our brains are, especially with memories. False memories are easily implanted. Our minds often remember what we want them to. So, you see, the wooden ship may have been on your dresser, or you may have just wanted it to be there. You needed it there so badly to fulfill the narrative you told yourself before you came here. But, never fear, we will dig much deeper into this in our next session and get much closer to the truth, I'm sure."

Wilbur raced home, more excited than ever. Although the doctor had been skeptical, he knew what he experienced while he was under. It was so vivid, far more than any dream or his imagination could conjure up. He could taste the salt on his lips, hear the pounding of the surf, feel the heaving in his stomach as the ship rode the seething waves. The explosion of timber on the rocks was ear-splitting. The unholy screams of the dying men, however, were something he never wanted to hear again.

Another sensation forced its way to the surface. Wilbur found himself strangely drawn to this ghost. He didn't understand it at all. It made no sense, but he felt so close to her.

He flew across the causeway and screeched to a halt beside the house. Wilbur knew he had to somehow talk to Susannah. At the very least, he would go to the lighthouse and try to put himself in a trance, recalling the words of Dr. Beckett. If he could do that, he would be open to her presence.

Flinging the door open, he noticed June coming out of the house, but he ignored her and hobbled across the grass to the lighthouse, his leg still quite painful. She called after him, but he dismissed her with a wave of his hand and kept going.

Once inside, he was greeted with the familiar damp stillness, as a soft, quiet breeze danced through the tower. He stood just outside the center point of the lighthouse, his back to the open door, facing the middle, where Susannah had appeared in his dream. Closing his eyes, he took a deep breath and tried to relax. It was all about the relaxation, recalling what the doctor told him. He wasn't asleep, just deeply relaxed and at peace.

Wilbur worked to clear his mind and make it ready for her. He took out the broken piece of glass he now carried with him all the time and rubbed it with his thumb. Breathing in and out a few times, he closed his eyes. He silently called to her. *Susannah? Are you here? Can you see me? It's true, what you said. I was—am the captain of the* Yarmouth. He paused, waiting for a response.

At that moment, the wind picked up, but it didn't sound like the usual moan. It was higher pitched than normal. He could just make out his wife's—was it his *true* wife's?—thin voice as it whisked around the interior.

With his eyes still closed, and his heart racing, he spoke out loud, eager to see if she responded. But also a little afraid. Everything he was experiencing was so out of the norm for him. He no longer knew what to expect. Didn't know what normal was anymore.

"Susannah," he said aloud. "It's me, Merritt. Your husband. It's true, everything you said. I went to see someone today. He helped me understand. It's hard to explain what he did, but you were right. I can hardly believe it, but I'm Merritt Holland. I'm the captain of that ship. And, just as amazing, you're my wife!" He rubbed his finger over the glass in his pocket, careful not to cut himself.

"Merritt, you're finally here. We can be together now. Whoever you saw today, I don't know how they did it, but I can see you and hear you. You believe. That's the most important thing."

A warm wave rippled through his body, unlike anything he'd ever sensed before. Wilbur sighed with contentment and peace, as a deep affection rose to the surface. It was a yearning for something unknowable up to this point.

"Susannah?"

"Yes, my dear husband."

"I don't know how to explain this," Wilbur said, his eyes still closed and his thoughts and emotions a maelstrom in his head.

"Just say what's in your heart."

"I think I'm in love with you—I always have been.

In my previous life, and this life, too. I felt it the first time I walked into the lighthouse. I just didn't know it at the time."

"Well, of course you have. We were destined to be together. And now we can be. For all time."

"Susannah, I'll do whatever you ask. I just want to be with you." Wilbur's breaths came more rapidly now as his heart beat faster. He could feel it pounding in his chest and his knees were shaking. He realized Susannah was his one true love. And now he had another chance at eternal happiness. "I want to hold you," he said, extending his arms to the center.

"Once you're in my realm, we can hold each other forever, my love."

"That would be heaven. You've brought me unimaginable joy, like I've never known before." Wilbur's voice was low as he confessed what was in his heart. He was reluctant to open his eyes, afraid to spoil the moment in case she wasn't there. But he could hear her voice, plain as day. It wasn't the wind, it wasn't his imagination. Susannah was here with him, just in some other dimension. Another realm, as she called it. He didn't try to understand it, just didn't want this moment to end.

"Soon. Very soon. We'll be together, just like I promised."

His chest filled, and long-buried feelings stirred. "That will be a magical time, you and me," he said. "When that time arrives, could I be so bold as to kiss you?"

Wilbur heard a scuffling noise at the door and whirled around, opening his eyes.

"Who will you be kissing, Wilbur Philpott?" June snapped, her voice low and angry. She looked around and leaned to the side to see behind him. "Who the hell were you talking to?" she demanded. She followed the path of the stairs, but they were empty. "Well?"

Wilbur whipped his head back around just in time to see some wispy fragments of fog dissipating from the center of the lighthouse. "*No!*" he cried. "What have you done?"

"What have *I* done? You're completely mad, you know that?"

His knees crumpled, and he moved to the steps to sit down. "She was right there," he moaned, his hand outstretched.

June marched over to him. "Look, I didn't see anyone. But so help me, if you're seeing someone and plan on leaving me, you've got another thing coming. This stupid lighthouse and that house," she said, pointing a thumb over her shoulder, "is half mine. And it's *all* mine when you kick off. And I'm not sharing it with anyone. Understand?"

Wilbur tilted his head back and stared at her. "That's what you're worried about? That's your main concern? The lighthouse?" He chuckled, and then laughed. "I'm chasing eternal happiness, and you're chasing a few dollars. You just don't understand, do you?"

"No, frankly, I don't. Your obsession with this place was mildly amusing years ago, then it became embarrassing, and now I think you're ready for the loony bin. Maybe if you see that shrink again, let him know I caught you talking to thin air."

"Dr. Beckett was quite helpful," he said, standing up. "I'm going again on Tuesday. With just my first session, I learned a lot. And next week, he promised to find out much more about me and this big, tall, beautiful lighthouse of mine." He emphasized the last word as he stepped around June and out the door.

CHAPTER FOURTEEN

It took a long time for Tuesday to roll around. Wilbur couldn't wait for his appointment with Dr. Beckett. This time, they wouldn't waste any time with the preliminary stuff. They would get right to it. Start with the age regression immediately.

June was gone more than she was at the house. At first it bothered him, but when he realized Susannah was his one and only, all the hurt that June had caused faded to the back of his mind.

Over the weekend, he had a couple of tourists show up to see the lighthouse, a duty he always enjoyed. He hoped the pride he felt for the historic tower came through for the folks who visited. He always tried to entertain and educate them, and he especially loved when children came. The joy on their faces was worth all the maintenance and upkeep it commanded.

Finally, Tuesday arrived. Wilbur arrived at Dr. Beckett's office and signed in at the front desk, making small talk with the receptionist. Soon after, he was ushered into the doctor's office and sat on the sofa.

"Mr. Philpott, how have you been?"

"Very well, Doctor, thank you." Wilbur sat with his hands on his knees, eager to get the small talk out of the way and to move forward with the trance.

"Before we get started, I hope you haven't been reading anymore Bridey Murphy stuff. It's important that you not be influenced by anything."

"No, not at all. I took the book back to the library. Haven't looked at it since I read it a week ago."

"Good." Dr. Beckett gestured for Wilbur to recline on the couch, which he did. "What I'd like to explore today is not so much the shipwreck, but your life before that. Your life with your wife." He looked at his notes and back to Wilbur. "Susannah, was it?"

"Yes, that's right."

"Why don't we begin? If you remember from last time, simply look at the brass star on the wall and focus on the sound of my voice. You're just going to relax, and I'll take you down those imaginary steps. You recall how we did that?"

"Yes," Wilbur said with a nod, already feeling the normal tension ease from his body as he sank into the sofa.

Dr. Beckett took him back decades at a time with each flight of stairs he descended, quicker this time than before. He paused when he had Wilbur right after birth and then took him beyond that time. Beckett guided him to a few years before the shipwreck and slowed down the regression, speaking in a relaxed tone.

"Can you tell me your name, please?"

"Merritt Holland."

"And you're the captain of a ship, is that right?"

"Yes," Wilbur said, his voice low but strong. "The *Yarmouth*, out of Halifax."

"Do you have a wife, children?"

"My wife is Susannah. She can't have children."

"I see," Beckett said. "Where are you now? What do you see? What's around you?"

"I'm waiting for Susannah to join me at the docks. I'm making the Liverpool run and she's going to join me, even though the crew doesn't like it." Wilbur frowned at the memory of that.

"Why doesn't your crew want your wife aboard?"

"Women are bad luck on a ship, anyway. But they say it's because she's a witch and can't be trusted. They're afraid of her, but she's always been friendly with them, and has never brought ill fortune to us."

"Is she a witch?" Beckett asked.

A reflexive denial almost escaped Wilbur's lips, but he paused. "I think so. I'm not sure. She's from Salem originally."

"Lots of people are from Salem and they aren't all witches," the doctor said.

"True," Wilbur murmured. "Still, the crew doesn't like her. I have to pay them extra when she's aboard."

"Tell me about your early life with her," Beckett said.

"We met in Providence and had kind of a whirlwind romance. I had just come back from San Francisco, through the canal, and up the east coast, and had the *Yarmouth* in dry dock. I knocked around Providence while I waited for the ship to be reconditioned. She was a barmaid in a tavern I frequented and, after a week of going in there, I asked her to a show. We hit it off right away and were pretty much inseparable after that." A small smile came to his lips, and he continued. "When the *Yarmouth* was ready, I asked her if she wanted to get married and come with me. She said yes and the next week we set sail for London, then Gibraltar, and Capetown. We traveled the world, she and I. We were deliriously happy."

"Tell me, did anything occur to lead you, or your crew, to believe she was a witch?"

Wilbur was silent for a few moments, but spoke again in a low voice. "There was a time when we were in London. I had hired a few new hands for the run to Gibraltar. One of the men tried to, well, have his way with her. I knew nothing about it, but we hadn't left port yet. The day we were to have departed, he never showed up to the pier. So the first officer and I went to his boarding house, not too far from the ship. We found him in his room. He had hanged himself. It was later that I found out he had tried to defile Susannah. Some of the men were saying she convinced him to do it. That she had a special mirror and could be very persuasive. If she stared at you, you could do things against your will. They always averted their eyes when she was around."

"I see. But you never experienced anything like this yourself with her?"

"No, never. We were in love."

"So you don't believe she was a witch, then?"

"No, I guess not," Wilbur replied softly.

"Tell me what happened after the shipwreck. What do you see?"

He took in a deep breath, and his face sagged. "The ship had grounded on the rocks and, after I broke through the cabin door, I ran to her. She was barely conscious. I scooped her up in my arms and ran to the side. The waves were pounding the boat and what was left of it was rapidly disintegrating. I didn't hear men screaming anymore. I couldn't really see much since it was so dark, but I dropped her off the side and I jumped in after her. Trying to keep her head above water as best I could, I made for the shore. The breakers were twenty feet high and the wind was howling. I finally made it to the small beach near the lighthouse." Wilbur gritted his teeth and clenched his fists.

"Go on," Beckett said. "Take your time. You're safe here, remember."

With another breath, Wilbur continued. "That damned drunken lighthouse keeper. We wouldn't have foundered if he had lit it."

"What happened after you came ashore?"

"I stumbled to the lighthouse with Susannah in my arms. Once inside, I laid her down on the floor and, that's when I saw the keeper, sitting on the steps. 'Help me!' I cried, but he was too drunk to move." He moaned with a long sigh. "I held her close, and she gave me something. A tiny mirror, small enough to hold in the palm of your hand. She said something but I couldn't understand. And then she died."

"What happened then?"

"I was enraged. I couldn't see straight. There was a black pit in my stomach that grew and took over my body. That lighthouse keeper murdered my wife. And my crew. Every last man. I charged up the steps and wrestled him out the window. He stole my heart from me. My wife was my heart. I was out of my mind with, and I guess I didn't know what I was doing. After that, I returned to my beloved. She was cold, still, unmoving. And I knew then I had no reason to live. Maybe I could, somehow, join her in death. I looked around the lighthouse and, just outside, in a toolshed, I found a long, thick rope. I had never considered anything like this before, but I'd never had my heart torn out like that night. My reason to live was gone, and I would probably hang for killing the lighthouse keeper, anyway."

"What did you do then?" the doctor asked, his voice still soft and steady.

"I climbed to the first landing, about thirty feet off the floor, and shimmied out along one of the iron crossbeams. When I got to the middle, directly over my beloved Susannah's body, I tied the rope off and then formed a noose." Wilbur's voice caught in his throat, but he continued, his voice barely above a whisper. "I put the noose over my head, kissed the mirror she had given me, and slipped off the beam."

"Before we go on, can you tell me what the date is?"

"Yes, it's March 23rd, 1898."

"And the time?"

"It's early morning, around 1:30."

"Now, do you remember what happened next?"

Wilbur frowned, trying to recall, and make sense of what came to mind. "Everything is dark. I can't see anything, but I'm wet, like I'm back in the ocean again. But the water's not cold. No, it's warm. And now it's light again. I'm having trouble breathing. I'm coughing. There are voices all around me. But I'm okay, I can sense it. I feel safe. I must be in heaven." He let out a half laugh at the thought.

"What's so funny about that?" Beckett asked.

"Well, I killed myself. Isn't that a direct ticket to hell?"

"Perhaps. Perhaps not. Why don't we move forward a bit? I'm going to have you imagine those steps in your mind again. Concentrate on my voice. Let's go up just one flight of stairs, exactly one year's time, and open the door at the top. Step through, and let me know what you see."

"I see a lot of people around me. I see my parents. There are aunts and uncles. And a cake with a candle. Everyone's trying to get me to blow it out, but I can't. My mother blows it out for me and everyone claps. And then they sing. It's a little overwhelming, to be honest. I don't think I like all the noise and commotion. After a time, my mother takes me into my room and puts me in my crib and I fall asleep."

"Very good," Dr. Beckett said. "Now then, I'm going

to bring you out of the trance, slowly, by counting to five. Focus on my voice and with each number, you'll feel yourself gliding up those stairs, through all the doors, and when I reach five, you'll be fully awake. One...two..."

As Dr. Beckett counted, Wilbur became aware of the couch, the smell of the leather, the ticking of the clock, and the other ambient sounds surrounding him.

"...four...five. You can open your eyes now. You're completely awake."

He opened his eyes and blinked a few times, then turned to the doctor with his mouth open. "I saw everything, doctor! Everything was so, so real. It's unbelievable." He pursed his lips. "What do you think now? Do you believe I was Merritt Holland in a previous life?"

"I'll reserve judgment for now, but yours has been a most interesting case. The details you recall are quite vivid, more so than other patients I've attempted this with."

Wilbur sat up on the couch and took some deep breaths. The memories of what he recalled while in the trance were overwhelming. He shook his head in amazement. As he stood, the doctor spoke up.

"I have a question, Mr. Philpott. What's your birthday?"

"My birthday? March 23rd."

"What year, please?"

"Eighteen ninety-eight."

The doctor nodded and made a note. "When you were recalling the final moments of your life as the ship's captain, I asked you what the date was. The date you gave me as Merritt Holland is your—Wilbur Philpott's—birthday."

Chills ran up the back of Wilbur's neck. He didn't know what to say, and just stood there, facing the doctor while his eyes got bigger.

"Do you know what time you were born?"

It took him a moment or two to process the question, but Wilbur shook his head. "Sorry, I don't."

"Could you find out? Check your birth certificate, perhaps, and let me know?"

Finally feeling validated, Wilbur nodded vigorously. "Absolutely. I'll check the moment I get home and call you."

CHAPTER FIFTEEN

Wilbur could barely breathe on his drive home. The revelations while he was under the age regression trance were astounding, and confirmed everything Susannah's ghost had told him in his dream, and the other day when he wasn't dreaming.

The moment he threw the truck in park, he raced into the house. "June! June!" he called. "Where are you?"

"I'm upstairs. What do you want?"

He ran to the bottom of the stairs and looked up at her scowling face. "Where's my birth certificate? I need to find it right away."

She didn't move from where she stood, just put her hands on her hips and leaned forward a bit. "What in the world do you need that for?"

"I have to check something. It's very important. Please—where is it?" Wilbur paced at the bottom of the stairs. "Can you help me look for it?"

June sighed, but stayed put. "Have you checked your Nana's desk? That's where everything seems to disappear to."

Wilbur snapped his fingers. "Good idea," he said, turning away from her and darting to the antique secretary desk. He pulled open the lid and sat down, yanking drawers open and rifling through various papers. He found a yellowed envelope at the bottom of one of the drawers and frantically ripped it open.

"You're practically hyperventilating," June said from behind him.

"Gah!" he yelled, jumping from his seat. "June, you scared me."

"What do you need your birth certificate for, anyway?"

He ignored her and slipped the brittle paper out of the envelope. "This is it!" He scanned the paper, squinting to read the faded cursive handwriting. Halfway down, he came to the date and time of his birth. He gasped and covered his mouth as he whirled around in his chair to face his wife. "June! Look at this...look at the time. One forty-four a.m."

"And that matters why?"

"Because I was born the moment Captain Holland died. And he—or I, I guess—said the shipwreck happened early in the morning. That's the proof I needed. June, I'm the cap—"

"Oh, for god's sake," she said, interrupting him with a wave of her hand. "I'm not listening to any more of this foolishness." She stormed off, shaking her head.

Had circumstances been different, Wilbur would

have been angry or even sad at her dismissal, but he didn't seem to care any longer. Right now, he needed to call the doctor.

Trotting over to the kitchen phone, he dialed Beckett's office. After telling the receptionist who he was and that the doctor was expecting him, his call was put through. "Doctor Beckett, I found my birth certificate. I was born in the hospital in Framingham and I have the time right here. It was 1:58 in the morning."

There was a long silence on Beckett's end.

"Doctor, are you there?" Wilbur asked.

"Yes, Mr. Philpott. After you left, I went to the library and used the microfiche to look up the newspaper article about the shipwreck. One of the articles that was recovered from the wreckage was the ship's log. The last entry Captain Holland made was March 23rd, 1898, at 12:40 in the morning. According to the article, his entry was very brief. It consisted of two words: 'ran aground.'"

Wilbur's blood ran cold and he inhaled sharply. "If the ship ran aground at 12:40, and I was born at 1:58, that's what, a little over an hour?"

"Which would be time enough for Holland to jump overboard with his wife, make it to shore, and then to the lighthouse, where she died. And for him to toss the lighthouse keeper out the window and then kill himself."

More goosebumps danced up and down his arms and neck.

Dr. Beckett continued. "I have to admit, I was skeptical at first, but it all fits. The timeline matches."

Feeling his knees shaking, Wilbur sat down at the table. He took deep breaths and stared off into the distance, through the window, and at the door of the lighthouse.

"Mister Philpott, are you there?"

"Yes, I'm here," he said, feeling similar to going under in Dr. Beckett's office. His voice grew quiet, his tone even. "Thank you, Doctor," he said, barely above a whisper.

As he hung up the phone, that same ultra-relaxed state washed over him, just like during the session earlier. He blinked a couple of times and closed his eyes. Out of the fog, broad horizontal lines took shape. He realized it was the imaginary staircase Dr. Beckett had him picture. Taking a step down, then another, and another, the relaxation overtook him. His breathing was slow and even as he rose from the chair.

June's voice barely penetrated as he stepped toward the door. "...you doing?"

He couldn't hear her anymore, and he opened the basement door. Leaning in, he lifted a rope from a hook just inside the stairwell and turned back.

Wilbur shuffled across the kitchen and stepped down through the door to the lawn. Feeling not only deeply relaxed, but keenly focused, he knew what he had to do. He had understood it days earlier, but was more committed to it than ever.

His name wasn't Wilbur Philpott. He was Merritt Holland. *Captain* Merritt Holland, of the *Yarmouth*. The woman named June, who called herself his wife, whose voice was now thin and reedy, was vanishing from his memory. What he heard loud and clear now was his *real* wife, Susannah. And his true wife was compelling him—propelling him—toward the lighthouse.

CHAPTER SIXTEEN

Susannah's voice rang clearly in his head as he unlocked the lighthouse door and stepped inside. Taking the stone steps slowly, he felt the rough texture of the thick rope between his fingers. He didn't need the support of the railing. He was strong, confident, and sure-footed.

"Merritt, thank you for this," Susannah said. "I'll be free of this place. Finally free. Your loyalty to me, and mine to you, is unquestioned. Be not afraid. You can do this."

He reached the first landing and sat on the step. With no hesitation, he slid across to the iron beam that stretched across to the other wall, meeting the other crossbeam in the middle. With his hands on the beam, he raised his weight and shifted it, then repositioned his hands and did the same thing, inching his way to the center.

"Thank you, Merritt. I've waited for this for so long. Thank you, my love."

After several minutes, he was at the intersection of the two rusty beams. They were fastened together with thick, ruddy colored nuts and bolts, four in total. He formed a loop in the rope and wound the end around and around, cinching it tight. Taking the other end, he tied it securely to the crossbeam, pulling on it to make sure it wouldn't come loose.

"Merritt, now is the time. You're giving me the ultimate gift. I will love you forever. Thank you."

With that, he slid off the beam.

The rope held, but the weakened beams failed. Nearly a century of exposure to salt had eaten away at the metal. The sudden jerk of his weight pulled the beams away from the walls, sending them—and him—crashing to the floor.

The sound of his tibia cracking reached his ear a split second before the pain. Confusion and shock jumbled his brain until the shooting pain registered. "Arrgggh-hh!" He screamed in torment and sat up instinctively to grab his shin. His left hand didn't move as it should and when he tried, he cried again in agony. Another scream penetrated his sudden torture, but it wasn't his voice. It was higher pitched and only lasted a moment.

Before he could give it another thought, his full agony set him writhing on the floor. He twisted and shook, any remnant of the self-induced trance now gone.

"June," he shouted. "June! Help me!" He screamed until he was hoarse, but he knew she wouldn't hear him over the noise of the surf, especially if she was inside. "June..." His voice grew weaker as his panic subsided. Despair took over as he kept calling his wife's name.

He wasn't sure how much time had passed, or if he had blacked out, but he heard the back door slam shut. "June!" Wilbur renewed his cries with vigor, desperately calling to his wife.

"What?" she yelled from somewhere on the lawn. "I'm heading into town."

"Help me! I'm hurt!" he screamed. "Don't go!"

June's silhouette appeared in the doorway. "Oh my god, what have you done?" she said, rushing over to him.

He pointed to his leg, shaking his finger in pain and exhaustion.

She touched his shin and he cried with renewed torment. Pulling his pant leg up, she gasped when she saw the bone protruding from an ugly gash. "I'll call the ambulance," she said, sprinting out of the lighthouse.

She returned with a towel to hold against the wound.

Wilbur screamed in pain as she pushed hard against his leg.

"A noose? Wilbur Philpott, what the hell were you thinking?" she said, unwrapping it from around his neck. Looking at the iron beams lying next to him, she shook her head. "You could have brought the whole damn thing down on top of you."

A few minutes later, the ambulance arrived. They

stabilized him, and he was soon on the gurney and speeding toward the hospital.

Several hours later, he emerged from the operating room and was taken to a room on the next floor. June was waiting for him with a scowl.

"Is this what that shrink you're seeing prescribed?" she asked, after the nurse and orderly helped him get settled into his bed and had left. "Hanging yourself?" she whispered, looking around.

Wilbur looked down at the cast on his left arm and the much larger cast covering his right leg. "It wasn't Doctor Beckett," he said with a defeated sigh.

"Then why in the world would you do something like this?"

"I can't explain it."

"Does this have something to do with you thinking you're this captain?"

He took a breath to gather his thoughts and tried to adjust how he lay, but winced in pain at the movement. "I know you think it's crazy, but I really am Captain Holland. He died the moment I was born. I'm the reincarnation of Merritt Holland. Doctor Beckett himself said that everything lined up. It all made sense."

"So how does killing yourself fit into it?"

Wilbur knew he couldn't mention Susannah and what her plans were for them once he was free of his current body. June would have him committed. "I don't know," he murmured. "I guess it was all too overwhelming."

June started to say something in response, but was

interrupted when an orderly brought a tray of food in. He wheeled the tray over and elevated Wilbur so he was at a better angle. "I scrounged up the last of the dinners for you," the young man said. "Meatloaf. Supposed to be pretty good. Let me know if you need anything." He left, leaving Wilbur to stare at the food. He wasn't hungry, but figured he should probably eat something.

"At least you didn't break your right arm," June said. "I'd hate to have to feed you."

He picked at the pressed meatloaf and mashed potatoes and had eaten about half when he finally pushed the tray to the side.

June looked out the window at the darkening sky. "All right. I'm going to head home. Is there anything you want me to bring you tomorrow?"

"Maybe my *Ellery Queen* magazine. It's on the side table in the living room."

She nodded and started to leave, but an older man in a white coat breezed into the room. He unhooked the chart from the end of Wilbur's bed and glanced over it.

"Wilbur? I'm Doctor Stiglitz."

"Nice to meet you, sir. This is my wife, June."

The doctor nodded to her and turned back to Wilbur. "How are you feeling?"

"I've been better."

"I'm sure. You took quite the tumble, apparently. At your age, you may want to just hire someone in the future to make those kinds of repairs to that structure. You're a lucky man."

Wilbur furrowed his brows and stole a quick look to June, who nodded slightly.

Doctor Stiglitz continued, speaking in a staccato tone, barely taking a breath between sentences. "The breaks were relatively straightforward, fortunately, and surgery went well. The casts will keep your arm and your leg immobile for six weeks. Then, after that, you may have to do some physical therapy on that leg. We'll see how it looks when we cut the cast off. The arm will be about the same, possibly longer. We should get you out of here tomorrow sometime. Any questions? No? All right. If the pain becomes too much, ring for the nurse. Have a good night." With that, he hung the chart back on the foot of the bed, turned, and left.

Wilbur sighed and sunk back into the uncomfortable bed. He knew sleep would not come easily tonight. Did the doctor say six weeks until the casts could come off?

June apparently was thinking the same thing. "Six weeks? Oh, my god. You're really putting 'for better or worse' to the test, aren't you?" she said, with no trace of humor. She shook her head and headed for the door. "Call me when they discharge you tomorrow."

CHAPTER SEVENTEEN

"It's been almost two months, Wilbur. I'm going out of my mind," June said as she sat down at the table with the chicken casserole. Scooping out two servings, she sat back in her chair and stared at the food.

"I know you've been doing a lot for me these last few weeks, June Bug, and I appreciate it."

A quick flash of anger passed over her face. "Doing 'a lot'? I've been doing everything for you. Your casts are off, you can get around better, you don't need me here 'round the clock."

He sighed, knowing she was right. He just wasn't confident in going up and down the stairs without her. Even climbing into bed was a struggle.

Wilbur hadn't been in the lighthouse until his casts had been removed, and then only a few times. Never once did he hear Susannah, or the familiar moans that he knew as the voice of the lighthouse. All he heard was the usual wind howling through the windows.

There were no messages in the wind, no thin voices, or apparitions. He wondered if Susannah was gone.

"Well, you're all fed now," June said. "You can watch TV tonight or read. You can sleep on the couch so you don't have to worry about getting up the stairs."

"I don't mind you going out with your friends, of course, June. I just wish you didn't have to stay overnight. Being alone, I just get a little nervous, that's all."

"Now, you don't want me driving back late at night from Boston, do you? I haven't seen the girls in months and we're celebrating Debbie's birthday, so it's best that I stay at her place. You can see the sense in that, right?"

"I suppose," he said, rubbing his face. "Might get a bit of weather later, so I guess it's safer to not be on the roads."

"There, see? You'll be fine and I'll be home in the morning." June ate a few bites and rose from the table, gathering her purse and small suitcase.

Wilbur finished his dinner slowly and put the dishes in the sink, propping his cane against the counter. He couldn't stay on his feet for too long and June had assured him they could keep 'til morning. Making his way gingerly to his recliner, he eased himself down and thumbed through the *TV Guide*, trying to decide if he should watch a show or do some reading. All the channels were showing reruns, so that made his decision an easy one. Solving a mystery with Ellery Queen would be his activity of choice for the night. He tossed aside the *TV Guide* and picked up the mystery magazine, flipping to the start of a new story.

The wind picked up a bit as the shadows grew longer. He glanced out the window at the branches tapping on the living room window. Perfect way to set the mood for the story he had begun of a hiker gone missing from the woods. Just one page in, and there were already two possible suspects, maybe more.

Wilbur was knee-deep in clues when the phone rang, pulling him out of the story. Thankfully, June had brought the extension phone from the upstairs bedroom and plugged it in here in the living room. He leaned over the arm of his chair and picked up the receiver.

"Hello?"

"Oh, hello, Wilbur," a woman's voice said. "This is Elaine. Is June there?"

Wilbur frowned. "June? Why, no. She's on her way to town—Boston. Something about a party with you girls."

"A party?" Wilbur could hear the confusion in the woman's voice, which puzzled him greatly.

"Yes, I think she said it was Debbie's birthday."

There was silence on the other end for a few moments until Elaine spoke up again. "Well, I guess I didn't get the invitation. Sorry to have bothered you, Wilbur. Goodbye."

Before he could say anything, the line went dead. He hung it up slowly, his face scrunched up. Shaking his head slowly, he picked up his magazine and resumed reading. Or at least tried. He found himself reading the same paragraph several times and finally put it down.

He leaned heavily on his cane and stood up, then hobbled over to the TV. After pulling the On/Off switch and waiting for it to warm up, he twisted the knob to one of the UHF channels. Happy to find a Western on, he settled back down in his chair, still not sure why June's friend sounded confused and was calling for her. She should have been there by now. He hoped nothing had happened to her on the road. Glancing out the window again, he could see that it was quite windy now, although there was no rain. He was sure she was fine and tried to put Elaine's call out of his mind.

It was dark out now, and the tree branch was still tapping and scratching across the window. The bright beam from the lighthouse rotated through the low-hanging clouds, and reassured Wilbur that all was right the world. Just as the movie got to the good part, the phone rang again, startling him in his seat.

"Hello," he said, picking up the phone.

"Wilbur. How are you, my friend?" the man's voice rang out.

"Hi Charlie. I'm fine. Just watching a Henry Fonda movie. You're calling kind of late. Everything okay?"

"Well," he started. "Everything's just fine with *me*," he said, emphasizing the last word in his response. "I don't know if everything will be okay with you, though."

"What do you mean by that?" Wilbur said, frowning into the phone.

"Is June there, by chance?" Charlie said.

Wilbur sensed a bit of mischief in his friend's voice and frowned again. "No, she's in Boston with some friends. What's this about, Charlie?"

"Boston? Hmm...that's strange. Because I just saw her with Max Benson down at the marina about an hour ago."

"What? You're crazy. She's in Boston at a girl-friend's birthday—" Wilbur paused, trying to gather his thoughts. "You say she was with Benson in town at the marina?"

"That's right. They were getting into his beautiful thirty-eight foot Chris-Craft. Looked like they were heading out for a sunset cruise."

"Now, Charlie. That isn't funny. She assured me she was heading to Boston."

"I'm just telling you what I saw, my friend. Believe me or not."

"I don't believe you. And I don't want to hear anything more about it. Do you understand?"

"Okay, Wilbur, okay. Enjoy your movie."

Wilbur hung up and took a breath while a flash of anger pulsed through his body. Was it true? Or was it just Charlie being cruel? He didn't know who he was angry at, June or his friend. Charlie must have been mistaken, because he would never tell such a hurtful lie.

It was almost ten o'clock and he'd seen the movie before, so he knew how it ended. He rose from the chair and shuffled over to the TV set, turning it off. With a deep sigh, he headed into the kitchen and to the back door. He watched the trees whipping in the wind, but still didn't see any rain. Deciding that the lighthouse would be the best place to do some thinking, he reached for his jacket inside the basement stairs.

Wilbur felt a couple rain drops on his way across the lawn to the lighthouse, but nothing too bad. Once inside, he turned on the interior light and looked up the steps. He hadn't been able to climb the stairs in two months and knew he shouldn't try. At least not to the top. But he grabbed a couple tools and stuffed them in his pocket, just in case he made it all the way. He might need to repair something while he was up there. He would stop at the first landing and look out the window, and just think for a while.

He nodded his head and approached the first step, the steep one. Planting his cane and grasping the railing with his other hand, he hoisted himself up with relative ease. He looked around with a smile, proud that he had made the first step with no difficulty. Leaning on the railing again and using the cane, he trudged up the next few steps. He stopped to take a breath. Determined to at least make it to that first landing, he stepped up and up. After several minutes, he finally arrived, and sat down with a plop.

Twisting around to face outward, Wilbur saw the trusty beam of the lighthouse shooting across the dark water and its whitecaps. The wind had picked up and was now sailing through the lighthouse, sending a chill through Wilbur's body. He cocked his head at the familiar sound, barely able to make out Susannah's voice. She wasn't gone after all! The anger that had consumed him earlier left his body, replaced by joy at her thin, reedy voice.

He closed his eyes and tried to relax like Dr. Beckett had done it. He pictured the brass star in the doctor's office in his mind, then the staircase. The more he relaxed, the louder Susannah's voice grew in his head. But he couldn't make out any words; she was still too faint.

"Susannah," he whispered. "Are you there?"

He heard nothing except the wind howling and the surf pounding on the rocks below.

"Susannah? Where are you?"

His voice was met with silence. The wind had died down. Sighing deeply with despair, Wilbur opened his eyes and looked around at the dimly lit interior. He turned his body back to face the window and heard a large metallic click come from above. He waited a minute, staring out onto the black water, and he realized then what was missing. The rotating light that shone as a secure beacon had gone dark.

CHAPTER EIGHTEEN

Wilbur rubbed his face, feeling the stubble from his beard on his palm. "Now what could have happened?" he said out loud.

The wind picked up again, roiling around and through the old lighthouse. He instinctively reached into his pocket and took out the piece of glass. He now had no trouble hearing Susannah's voice this time. No trance or dream was necessary.

"Put the mirror on the step beside you."

He looked in his palm at the jagged glass and did as he was told.

"Someone has to die to free me, Wilbur." Her voice was tight and angry. "You bungled it the first time, so I'm taking matters into my own hands."

He gasped as a wispy apparition appeared in the center of the room. When the mirror fragment floated to the middle of the floor, his eyes grew wide and he covered his mouth.

"I don't understand any of this," he said. "I thought

we were to be together." He looked down the stairs to the floor, where Susannah hovered over the mirror. "And wait—you called me Wilbur." He started to get up when he heard a terrific crash on the rocks. It was more than the surf. It was heavy, like a tree being hit by lightning and splitting in two.

He whipped his head around and peered out the window. It was dark without the light, but he thought he saw something large teetering on the boulders. Something coming apart with each powerful wave.

He heard laughter coming from below, and it chilled him to the bone. It was an evil, raspy laugh, rattling and shaking. Turning his head slowly back around, he saw Susannah, not as a translucent apparition, but whole and fully formed. She was dancing 'round and 'round on the spot directly below the noose.

His eyes were transfixed by what he saw, disbelieving it. Wearing a blue waterlogged dress, Susannah whirled around, her arms outstretched and her head tilted back, laughing, shrieking with joy.

When he heard another splintering of wood on the rocks, he gazed out the window again, but couldn't make out anything solid. "I've got to get that light back on," he said, trying to get to his feet.

More laughter from below reached his ears. "You're not going anywhere, Wilbur."

"But I think someone's run aground. Could be people hurt."

With another peel of laughter, Susannah answered. "That's my hope!" She continued dancing, her feet stepping over the other as she swayed and spun, always staying directly in the center of the lighthouse floor.

"I have to try," Wilbur groaned, trying to lift himself again. He tried to hoist himself up with his cane, but it was no use. He was planted in place, unable to move.

"I told you, old man, you're staying put," Susannah said with crackling laugh and a twirl.

Struggling to understand what was happening, Wilbur then heard screams coming from the water, close to shore. He twisted his torso around to peer out the window, but it was too dark to see anything. He frantically tried to stand, but failed as Susannah continued to dance and laugh.

The screams died out, but Wilbur was in a frenzy trying to get up. He had to try to make his way to the edge of the water to help, or at least call someone.

He heard a commotion at the door of the light-house and whirled around to see June burst in. She was soaked and her clothing torn. Her hair was wild, and she was gasping for breath. Covered in sand and bits of seashell, she had obviously dragged herself along the small beach from the water.

She glared at Wilbur with fury in her eyes. "Why did you turn the light off? We ran aground because we couldn't see anything. We didn't know how close we were to shore. Max is hurt. He's hurt bad. You damned fool!"

"Max? Max Benson?" Wilbur screamed, pointing to the water. "You're on his boat? I thought you were with your friends in Boston. What the hell is going on, June?" He noticed Susannah was gone, but he could still hear faint laughing amidst the howl of the wind.

"What does that matter? Max is hurt, I'm telling you. He can't hold on much longer. Why are you just sitting there?"

"I can't move. My legs are—"

"Oh, shut up. Call the rescue squad. They have to get Max off the rocks. I think there are other boats out there, too. They're going to hit the rocks." She charged up the stairs toward Wilbur. "If you won't turn the light back on, I will," she said as she flew past him. "Call someone!" she shrieked.

"You lied to me, June. You told me you were with Debbie. I trusted you."

"Now's not the time, Wilbur! Are you going to call the rescue squad or do I have to do everything?" she screamed, halfway to the top. "You're pathetic!"

"I can't believe you lied to me. Charlie was right," Wilbur said quietly, shaking his head. June was out of earshot, but he could hear her footsteps receding as she approached the top. He sat, stunned at the truth of it. Blinking the tears back, he shifted on the stone step and ran his hands over his pants, clanking the pliers and screwdriver in his pocket.

He hadn't believed Charlie, but maybe he just didn't want to. But now it all made sense. The long and frequent trips into town June had made, the furtive phone calls, the way Benson had acted around him, it all added up. Did she ever love him? he wondered. She had to have, at least in the beginning. But when did it all fall apart? Was it buying the lighthouse when he retired? He just couldn't put his finger on it, but she probably didn't wake up one morning hating him. But she sure acted that way now.

"What the hell is the matter with this switch?" June screamed from the top. "It won't budge!"

Her voice barely registered with Wilbur. The humiliation at knowing his wife was sleeping with Max Benson raged inside him. If Charlie knew, the whole town probably did. And he was in the dark the whole time. When he recalled Susannah's promises, he felt even more ridiculous. She was a ghost, a witch, who had somehow gotten inside his head. And persuaded him to try and kill himself. Was she even real, or was it all his mind playing tricks on him?

Wilbur's shoulders sagged as the double betrayal struck him with as much fury as the waves. June had lied to him and Susannah? She cared nothing about him. Just wanted to be free. She had used him.

He sat and thought and brewed. The howling wind blew through the lighthouse as lightning flashed outside. June never loved me. Susannah either. A bile of despair and self-loathing rose from his stomach.

A metallic squeaking sound interrupted his brooding. It came from below him somewhere, but he couldn't make it out. Then he saw the bolts holding the iron railing into the stone unscrewing. One by one, they rotated outward and fell to the steps. Seven in all. His mind flashed back to something that had happened weeks ago, before he tried to hang himself. Looking at the iron railing, he wondered. Wondered why June didn't act more horrified about how close he had come to dying on the steps when the railing had become loose. She had seemed pretty nonchalant about the whole thing.

But how in the world did these bolts just unscrew by themselves? He swallowed as he realized he had not imagined everything after all.

A flash of blue caught his eye from below. Susannah was grinning, laughing at him, mocking him.

"Susannah," Wilbur moaned. "I'm your husband, Merritt. I thought we were going to be together."

"Merritt?" Susannah laughed with a loud cackle and twirled around, her blue dress billowing out from her body. "You're such a fool, Wilbur."

"But I was reincarnated! You told me, and the doctor confirmed it."

"Ha! You're so gullible. That was all made up, created out of whole cloth. I needed you—or anyone—to die so I could escape this place forever. I don't care who it is."

Wilbur's mind reeled. Was everything just a coincidence? His being born when the captain died? And maybe the doctor was right, that he had filled in the details that he wanted to remember during his sessions. He shook his head, while a shadow of despair settled over him.

"Finally!" June cried from above.

Wilbur looked to the top, then back to Susannah, who clapped her hands in delight.

"Your wife will oblige me in just a moment!" she exclaimed with another evil laugh.

The light came back on, rotating around like normal, a signal of safety along the rocky shore. Wilbur heard June muttering to herself as she slammed the door to the electrical room shut.

Above him on the stairs, he sensed her coming into view. She stood above him and shouted. "You haven't moved one inch! I told you to call the rescue squad. You idiot! God, I hate you!" She screamed at him as she continued down the stairs, holding onto the railing.

At that moment, another scream was heard coming from the rocks. A man's voice. It was hard to make out over the surf, but it was a frightened, mournful cry.

"Max! I'm coming!" June shouted, rushing past Wilbur.

"June, no!" Wilbur cried.

She took her hand off the railing to step around him, then grabbed on again, leaning on it hard as she rushed down the steps.

With a groan, and no bolts to hold it in, the railing let go from the wall. June lost her footing and somersaulted down the stone stairs. Her head hit the brick wall with a sickening thud as her arms flailed, bouncing off the steps.

She landed at the bottom of the stairs in a heap, with an arm twisted backwards. Her body faced sideways, but her head was bent upward, eyes open, unblinking.

In that instant, Susannah held the broken mirror over her head and shouted a string of unfamiliar words, *"Ana hurr, ana hurr! Faltahbes hathihi alemra'a ila l'abad!"*

The wind howled again through the lighthouse, transforming Susannah's solid form into a blue-white wisp which blew out through the door with a final, cascading laugh.

At the same time, Wilbur watched in amazement as a million ash-like particles swirled from June's body, spiraling high into the tower of the lighthouse. There was a deafening, mournful shriek.

"Noooo!" he heard June's voice cry, the wail coming from all around him. The unholy scream echoed within the lofty tower as the ashes billowed and twisted in long ropes.

Suddenly finding that he could stand, Wilbur rose from his step, his eyes wide as he tried to focus on his wife's lifeless form. The color had faded from her skin and her lips were a sickly shade of blue.

"June?" He knelt beside her and nudged her arm. He pulled his hand back when he encountered her cold skin. It wasn't even room temperature—it felt almost frozen. Wilbur rose to his feet and stood as the maelstrom of June's hollow screams and black particles continued, not fading or lessening in intensity, even as he stepped over her body and shut the door behind him.

Wilbur waved to a station wagon pulling up the drive. When they parked in front of the lighthouse, he trotted over to greet them. It was a cool, blustery day, with dark clouds racing across the sky. The mother and father pulled their jackets tighter and bundled up their two kids against the wind.

After his opening spiel about when the lighthouse was built, how many bricks it took, and how many steps to the top, he led them inside. "Are there any questions before we head up?"

"You're the lighthouse keeper?" the man asked.

"That's right," Wilbur replied. "Been here for, gosh —a long time now." He rubbed his whiskers with a smile.

"I didn't think lighthouses had keepers anymore. No offense."

"None taken. We're kind of a dinosaur anymore. There are still a few manned lighthouses around. Most are automated now. And I'd fight to stay on here, but the state has it scheduled for demolition next spring. They say the salt spray has done too much damage, and it's not safe. I was hoping to see it to its centennial, but they're telling me there's no way. But ninety years is pretty good, I think. She'll be ninety next year, 1971. That'll make me seventy-three, so I guess I'm doing pretty good, too."

The man smiled at Wilbur and his family. "Glad we got here when we did, kids. Let's have the honor of a tour, if we may," he said to Wilbur.

"My pleasure. Now watch that first step and hold on to the railing."

When they arrived at the first landing, he invited them to sit down, but not to crawl toward the open window. He gazed at the two children, both girls, who seemed to be around ten or twelve years old.

The wind picked up, and the mother shivered.

"We won't stay here too long, I promise," Wilbur said. "We'll get up the stairs in a moment and out of the wind. But while we're here, I want you to listen carefully, for the lighthouse is haunted. Can you hear that sound, just beneath the wind?"

The girls gasped in unison and leaned forward, straining to hear the noise. "We don't hear anything, Mister," one girl said.

"Oh, it's there all right," he assured them. "Let me call to her." Wilbur stood on the step above the landing and looked to the center of the lighthouse, cupping a hand to his mouth. "June Bug, we have some visitors."

A raw, angry roar whipped through the tower,

through the family, and swirled around Wilbur so hard it knocked him backward into the wall. He gripped the railing tightly so he wouldn't fall.

The girls' eyes went wide and one of them put a hand to her mouth in shock.

"Now, June Bug, don't be rude to our visitors."

ACKNOWLEDGMENTS

I had such fun writing this story, but as with all my books, it was a team effort. My beta readers were instrumental in pointing out inconsistencies with the timeline and places where the story dragged a bit. They each provided amazing feedback and encouragement. It is my fervent hope that I have provided as much assistance to the following authors in their journey as they have in mine: Dana Hawkins, Lisa Thomas, Elley Fletcher, Elysia Strife, Allison Ray, and Kristen Hornung (who graciously agreed to multiple readings of the manuscript).

Thanks also to Nadia Sakkal, another author friend, who supplied the Arabic translation found in Chapter 18: "*Ana hurr, ana hurr! Faltahbes hathihi alemra'a ila l'abad!*" for "I'm free, I'm free! Imprison the woman forever!"

As always, I'm indebted to Ryan Harrison for his editing skills and fact-checking prowess. He's excellent at finding the smallest of plot holes and keeping me honest when I try to stray too far from reality with my facts. It's always a little nerve-wracking receiving a manuscript back from my son, but I know he's just as nervous having to edit one of my books, petrified that it would be really bad and he wouldn't have the heart to tell me.

Finally, thank you to my wife, Paula, for her unwavering love and support, through five books now. I feel incredibly lucky to have such a cheerleader. There are many more to come, which means more evenings that she has control of the TV. ;-)

ABOUT THE AUTHOR

R.W. Harrison is a marketing professional residing in Florida. In addition to his novels, he has had works published in the *Tampa Bay Times* and *Going Places* Magazine.

He also works as an editor, book cover designer, and formatter.

He has taught courses to first-time novelists and is always eager to help new writers.

If you liked this book, please leave a review on Amazon, Goodreads, or your favorite review site.

Connect with the author through his website or social media:
www.rwharrisonbooks.com
www.facebook.com/RWHarrisonAuthor
www.instagram.com/robertharrison_author